BLOOD ECHOES

Twins always finish each other's sentences.
Especially in prison.

Published in 2026, Edition 1.

eBook ISBN # 9781965372777
Paperback ISBN # 9781965372784
Hardcover ISBN # 9781965372791

Edited by CM LLC. Published independently.

Cover & interior art by Aaron Ryan & CM LLC.

For Sweeps, Bren & AJ:
my true loves.

-

Thank you for loving me through my peace
and my horror.

CHAPTERS

"He who has rejected his demons badgers us to death with his angels."

- Henri Michaux

NOTE ON AI

Unfortunately, or fortunately, we live in an age of AI.

Every day, more and more services spring up promising revolutionary and innovative results using artificial intelligence. The authoring industry is not immune to this.

I want every one of my readers to know that not once did I employ, nor will I *ever* employ, the use of AI to sculpt any part of any of my stories. Those who know me know that I am staunchly and adamantly opposed to such cheats.

I'm very proud to be a verified human. The ability to create is a gift that I was endowed by my Creator, and I will never forfeit that nor set it aside to propagate something synthetic and imitative.

Everything you've read by me in this novel, and in my other works, is 100% entirely created by me, the genuine article. I'm a verified human and always will be.

To my fellow authors, I urge you to preserve the sacred gift of human creation and never stoop to such lows. Always cherish this gift you've been given. If you encounter writer's block, take a break. Don't cop out. Don't take the road more traveled by. Don't cheat. Toe the line for all of us, and keep creation – *true* unadulterated creation – alive.

Long live humanity.

Also, if you're an author – or even a budding one – I'd love to personally extend an invite to you to join me in a unique group on Facebook: the *Authors & Writers ONLY* group of which I am the admin. This group is one where you can connect with thousands of other authors across the globe, ask questions, learn and grow as a writer, and network.

Grapes grow best in bunches, after all. ☺

Keep it up. This dream of authoring is *so* worth it. Keep your humanity as you do so. God bless you as you use the gift of creation to sculpt your stories. May they, and you, be utterly successful.

Sincerely,

Aaron Ryan,
Verified Human

JOIN ME!

You are cordially invited to join me in my private and exclusive Facebook group.

This is a group where no scammers nor spammers are allowed, where you'll find information about upcoming releases, news on my screenplay adaptations, discount codes, giveaways, and, for authors, encouragement and tools. I hope to see you there! Visit: authoraaronryangroup.com (the link will forward you to Facebook).

Thank you so much.

PART ONE: THE BRICKERTS

NOTE: Carefully observe the dates following each chapter heading. There are two running timelines: one from August 2020, and one from January 2021. (The past timeline is in italics.) With this clarification, you'll better understand the complete story. Enjoy *Blood Echoes*!

1: THE NOW

Present: **Monday, January 4th 2021**

I never said I was guilty, but that doesn't make me innocent, either.

The whole experience is something that I would never wish upon anyone, not even those I've despised.

And there have been many of those. *Many.*

Being a security guard wasn't my first choice for a career. Not in a million years. Not after the Marines. It isn't something I'd wish on my worst enemies. It's provided a cesspool of people to despise; a melting pot of abominable individuals; a revolting horde of detestable sub-humans and people that should never have been born.

There are the thieves, the rapists, the murderers, the armed robbers, and their ilk.

Then you have the cyberstalkers and embezzlers and blue-collar criminals and their type.

And finally, you got those guys who seem sweet at first, like they wouldn't harm a fly, you know? Those are the worst. They lull you into a false sense of security because they seem so innocuous, so neutral and anodyne. But just when you're starting to let your guard down, you catch them on a bad day, and that's when they strike, surprising you with a toxic brew of horrific violence and repressed emotions.

Elias Brickert was one such guy.

I'll always remember the day the guards brought him in, and he was strip-searched and had his intake just like the rest of the meatheads at Airway Heights Corrections Center. He was processed, got his number, and was given his cell in medium custody, shared with inmate 8771632, Trenton McAllister.

McAllister didn't last long in the cell with him.

Sure, Elias said he was innocent. Maybe, in the end, he was. Maybe he truly didn't do what he was convicted of. But history tells another story, and so do forensics.

Blood never lies. Fingerprints don't tell tall tales. Strands of hair don't exaggerate. Blood, fingerprints and hair were all present at the scene with one Elias James Brickert, and that was enough to convict this guy and send him to the slammer for two life sentences, consecutive. Not that concurrent would even matter.

Elias was an attractive man. I say 'was,' because he's dead now. His identical twin brother, Gabriel Titus Brickert, isn't… but I don't ever want to see him again. *Ever.* Creepy as all get out. He was like Elias, and unlike him. Someone killed Elias' cellmate. And someone killed many others there. They say it was Elias, but I'm not convinced. I'm still not entirely sure he did, but I don't even care anymore. I know the truth, but I've had to let the truth go and move on. All of it – *all* of it - was the most gruesome and unnerving experience I've ever had, and I don't ever want to lay eyes on anything that evil again.

How could he have done all that from his cell? I sigh and shake my head. I've more or less stopped wondering. I know now. But the thing is, I have bigger fish to fry and better people to love.

Better people such as Lela. She's twelve, and that's a basket of emotions all wrapped up in a burgeoning combination of glittering nail polish and raw angst. She needed me through all of it, and I wasn't there for her. Never again. I love my daughter, and I'll be there for her now.

But there was one more that I loved… and the sad reality is that it was Elias himself.

Did I love him? Yes, I did. Or, at least, the part of him that I remember being human. It's a long, dark tale of confusing teeter-tottering, manic swings, and dark interludes permeated with alternate personalities and demons. I don't talk about it much anymore because…what's the point? It's all over now.

Or, at least, I think it is.

With demons, you never really know.

Tomorrow's the deposition. I don't want to go, never did. But the powers that be still hold sway, and, though I no longer work at Airway, I'm a witness, answerable to the courts for what happened there, and I have memories, regardless of what I look like or who I am.

I saw both of them… and what they both did.

I'm not even sure they're going to believe my story, but I can't even tell them the full truth. Besides… that's where the luxury of the security cameras works in my favor. Don't believe me? Check the tapes. Tapes also don't lie. Not blurry, gritty, grainy tapes un-doctored by AI and cheap CGI tricks. I saw them myself, and so did they.

The days of Airway Heights are behind me, and for that, I'm grateful. There was no air there, and there was no way out. It was inaptly named: we weren't on the heights. We felt like we were in the depths of depravity and hell the entire time. All of us guards did. The inmates too.

You know those times where something just feels tangibly wrong, but you just can't put your finger on it, but it's in the atmosphere around you, and the air is so thick you can chew it? That palpable sense of unease and lack of peace.

That was Airway Heights for me in the summer of 2020. As if we didn't have enough to contend with Covid-19, then we have the case of Elias Brickert on all our hands, and it was something I will never ever forget.

The things I saw…

The sounds I heard…

The things that happened to those inmates.

And the things that happened *outside* these walls. They defied belief. All of them. Dr. Eggers really helped; I'll give her that… but there are things that are definitely beyond the purview of your average shrink, and, though I appreciate her demeanor and her approach, she couldn't put a label on any of it either.

Except *unexplained.*

She and her 'pastor partner' work inside Airway. Her partner is Pastor Rosie Campion. They're both nice, I suppose, but I'm glad my days on the wireframe *un*-comfy couch of Dr. Penelope Eggers are over, and the staunch prayers of her devoted pastor friend Rosie haven't driven away the dark at night, or silenced the whispers that still haunt my dreams. I've seen and learned too much.

Because, when you get right down to it, I had a part to play in everything that went down, and I was compelled to do things that no guard there – or *anywhere* – should ever have to. *Ever.*

I just hope I make it through the deposition tomorrow and that I can grab a nice burger afterwards. And a smoke too, as long as I can get away with it without Lela noticing. I haven't been able to eat since Thursday. Good thing Lela's got an appetite. But she didn't see what I saw.

I take a deep breath to eject the weight off my lungs: the weight that seems to be compressing me into a stifling box daily. The weight that's going to return with a vengeance tomorrow as I sit there and desperately try to get their sharp, pointed questions answered as quickly as possible so I can get the hell out of there and dress up my burger.

One more sigh as I clench my eyes closed and shut out the demons. Or at least try to before I lay back down and venture another desperate attempt at sleep. It was never this way in the military. But it is this way now. Insomnia is even worse than demons sometimes.

After all, I won't say I'm completely innocent, but I'm not exactly… *not* guilty.

2: THE THEN

The Past: ***Tuesday, July 21st 2020***

He's cute, this one.

Not exactly my type, with all those scars – or whatever they are – on his arms. And chest. And neck. And legs. And everywhere. But… whatever. I wish that mask didn't cover half of his face, because I'd love to see all of it.

He's got lanky brown hair and a solid build under that jumpsuit. Grizzled, that five o'clock shadow is really starting to show. Couldn't have been a nice ride all the way from King County Jail. Can't blame him for not being able to shave yet. I'm sure he'll clean up nicely.

I need to make this quick because my shift ends in 15 minutes. I hate these intakes as I'd much prefer to be roaming the grounds and making sure these yahoos stay in compliance and out of trouble. That's where my military training makes me feel safer than Betty, Janice or even Big Shirley. Shirley is ex-military too, but she's lost touch with who she is, and she doesn't remember even simple stuff like high-impact strikes to vulnerable areas like eyes, throat, groin, knee strikes, or even double-leg, steering wheel technique, stuff like that. She's getting old and crusty. I fear for that one.

But this guy? *Brickert, Elias James* is what his file reads. Age 33, same as me! Grew up in North Bend, Washington, moved to Seattle, and that's where the crime took place. Second-degree murder and conspiracy to commit murder. Conspiracy with *whom* I don't know. Right now, it doesn't matter, because he's here, and I've got to process him. I look him over quickly, before returning to his prisoner intake folder. Seems easy enough, and his file reads straightforward: mother and father passed, only a twin brother on the outs named Gabriel. No other biological family members.

His tattoos are weird. They look like protective sigils or something. I've seen those kinds before, I mean, we get all kinds of characters in here. One guy was so marked up with these things that he looked like a freaking black raccoon. They called him 'black rac' in here for a while. Dude was white – or so they say – but you would never know it. Those eyes. They were white as a soft, quiet snow and reached out for you with a devilish iciness. But these marks covering Elias Brickert are more patterned, nuanced. They look like something out of the occult, like protective sigils, if you ask me.

I'm no expert, but I've seen enough TV, and I remember something on the X-Files or whatever it was. These look like those. His file says his brother has a lot of the same marks, tattoos, whatever, faded from childhood. Hope we don't ever mix them up and bring the wrong guy back in, *yuk yuk yuk...*

But maybe Gabriel is as cute as Elias.

"Vossler! Hey – Tracie! You wanna speed this up?" Cathcart shouts with a repugnant grin that I can totally make out behind his mask. I hate that guy, but he's also a friend. It's like he reads my mind and knows when I get the hots for some dude in here. Maybe he was a clairvoyant in another life. I'll have to ask Dr. Penny what she thinks about that kinda crap.

"Yeah, yeah," I bark back. "Shut it, Howard." I sit down and briefly pour over the last bits of info in this guy's file. Different from the last one, but same as him. And he'll be just as different and just as same as the next inmate I process in here. A criminal, with his own particular crime and rap sheet, his own particular habits, hurts and hang-ups. But he's still a criminal, and this is where he'll stay until the end of his days.

I fear for him. He's cute. And you just *know* someone's gonna wanna mess up that pretty face. With a shake of my head, I close the file roughly and motion to McFarland to bring him in. He's cuffed. I'll be fine. I toss one more contemptuous grin over at Cathcart. "That one's for free, butthead," I say, and he scoffs, shakes his head, and moves on.

One last peek at the file while McFarland has Brickert sit in front of me. The pungent aroma of BO hits me hard, and my eyes flicker up to the beefy man in front of me in his prison regulation orange jumpsuit. He manages a weak smile.

Maybe underneath all those tattoos is a softy.

Careful, Tracie, I chide myself. *Don't melt too early.*

Brickert studies me for a second, like he's got ears inside my head.

"Alright, Brickert, nice to meet you," I manage, with my best *I'm-friendly-but-we'll-never-be-friends* face. "Did you get everything you need for your cell?"

He nods quickly.

"Alright. You got Number 9254381. Nuttin' lucky about that, but memorize it, k? He take his photos?" I ask, flicking my head up McFarland. The guard nods.

"Alright, good. Any allergies, special diets, gluten-free stuff we should know about?"

"Uh, no, thank you."

Hmm. Nice voice. Gravelly. Stop it, Tracie.

"Alright, good. Any meds?"

"Uh, yes," he says quickly. "Risperidone and olanzapine. 2 milligrams daily each."

Anti-psychotics, I think to myself. *Great. Okay, so he's cute but weird.* Suddenly his cuteness factor plummets. Those are for paranoid schizophrenia and other nice dispositions, hallucinations, anxiety, all that. Wonderful.

Still, I nod politely, recording it down. "We'll take care of it. Any other special needs?"

"Uh, when can I see my brother?"

"Guard for your section'll brief you on all that. Orientation for Medium Custody is pretty brief. You'll find out visiting hours and all that. It's different for each block, and it's different for minimum security and work crew. K?"

"Alright, thanks," he says, softly, resigning himself to not knowing everything yet.

"Anything else?"

He shakes his head vigorously, and tufts of his lanky hair fall back into his face, masking his eyes. He's got nice eyes.

Tracie! Enough already.

"Alright. McFarland is the guard for your block for now, but they got a rotation I'm not familiar with. He'll keep you posted on the names of the other guys and you'll get acquainted. Your cellie," -here I peek back down at my logs and search for Brickert's name- "yeah, he ain't here yet but you'll meet him soon." I glint at him, but I can't hide a bit of a mischievous smile behind my mask. "Be nice, eh?"

He smiles back weakly. "Yes, ma'am."

"Alright. Good luck," I say, and that's it. McFarland motions for him to get up and start heading back to the line for all those heading to Medium Custody, R building.

As for me, I'm heading home to my daughter. But first, a burger on the way. I can't shake his face as I hang up my hat and stuff my locker, grabbing my keys and shouting a *see-ya-tomorrow* to Marge at the front.

Such a nice face.

He was cute, that one.

3: THE QUESTIONS

Present: **Tuesday, January 5th 2021**

This place is stuffy, and I hate it already.

And I don't like this guy, this Mitch Landon court reporter or deposition reporter guy, whatever he is, with his snotty questions and his over-the-glasses piercing glare and his repugnant overage of cologne. Reminds me of the time I felt like I was interrogating somebody unjustly, peppering them with all these questions and making them squirm. Now I know how it feels.

The questions are getting harder and more pointed, and someone is obviously behind this puppet, trying to put me on the spot. He's clearly got some kind of agenda, and I wonder if he's been paid by someone in the system. These guys are supposed to be neutral, but his snide looks and muttered comments speak volumes.

I knew I should have retained an attorney. Glad I spoke to those Avvo attorneys before this; I gleaned what I could as far as how to handle this deposition and keep myself out of trouble.

"Would you like to take a break?" Mitch asks me, numbly and completely devoid of empathy.

"No," I say, flatly.

"Fine. Let's continue," he says, and the room settles a bit. It's only him and me in here. Well, and his ego takes up all the other chairs, leaving only the floor for my pride.

I count the seconds. Thirty-four go by before he even 'continues.' He's staring at his own notes the entire time. Maybe he doesn't have the compute power to keep track of where he was. At least those precious seconds allow me to take a deep, frustrated breath and let it out audibly like a bubbling cauldron of discontent.

"Keeping you from something?" he asks, punching keys into his laptop and not meeting my eyes.

"Yes. I need to get my nails done," I stab.

The faintest flicker of a sly grin teases at the corner of his lips as he types. Finally, his fingers slow to molasses and he looks up and resumes. “Okay.”

“Okay,” I agree coldly.

“On the night of August 2nd, do you know where the inmate Elias Brickert was?”

“He should have been in his cell, like the rest of them. At least, he was there at first.”

“And what happened at 8:03pm?”

I flick my eyes around. I’ve already covered this. “What I heard was that he was suddenly not there. That’s when the staff alarm went off and everyone was told to report to R building.”

“And is that where Trenton McAllister was in the cell with Elias Brickert?”

“So I’ve heard. Except Elias was apparently no longer there in his cell.”

“And when you say he was no longer there, where did he go?”

“Asked and answered,” I say, using the Avvo attorney’s recommended phrase.

“Can you elaborate please?”

I sigh, and though I try to control it, my head shakes in frustration. “I said this already. They said he was no longer there, and no one knows where he went. He disappeared.”

“He wasn’t anywhere else on the grounds?”

I stare icily at him. If my eyes could shoot stalactites into his stupid frown, they would. “Isn’t that what *disappeared* means? Come on, man. I’ve been here for seven hours already.

Your repeating questions are starting to run circles around each other."

"Please cooperate. I'm just trying to do my job and get the full record," he grunts mechanically, devoid of pathos. I scoff. "For the record, please state where you believe inmate Elias Brickert went."

"For the record, *Mitch,* I do not know where he went. He simply disappeared. That's what I heard."

"I see," Mitch says with a patronizing air of clinical snootiness. "And who did you hear all this from?" he pries.

"Asked and answered," I grunt once more.

"So, in your opinion, an inmate in Medium Custody vanished into thin air straight through cinderblock walls and climbed a razor-wire fence, escaping Airway Heights Corrections Center on October 12th."

"Sure," I fire nearly instantaneously, sensing his entrapment and sarcasm. "Go with that."

"Ma'am, I just-"

"Look, Mitch, you're a court reporter, right?"

"Of course."

"Good. Just checking. Because this 'prosecuting attorney' act you're trying to pull off just comes across like a cheap hustle. Why don't you drop it?"

He just stares at me with a stupid condescending grin, and it's all I can do to restrain my ex-military training from slapping it off his rosy friggin' cheeks, not that my body is anywhere the shape it was in during my stint in the Marines. I long for the days… I'd take care of him.

"Fine. Let's get back to your knowledge of-"

"Knowledge of *what*?"

"Of the incidents at Airway Heights, of course."

"Do you think *I'm* responsible?"

"It's not my place to-"

"That's right. It isn't. So, Mr. Court Reporter, why don't you just ask the questions without all the attitude. It's getting old."

"I can do that."

"Great."

"Great. So, back to the main situation, it seems as though, according to the authorities," -here he reads from a report below him- "Guard Tracie Vossler may have covered for Mr. Brickert in the murder of Mr. McAllister." He stops reading, and returns to me. "The plaintiffs would like to know if you had anything to do with his disappearance, on the record."

At this point, since he's clearly insane, I decide to give up, throwing my hands up in the air and rolling my eyes noisily. "Sounds like a great story, Mitch. Run with that, since that's the narrative you've all decided to run anyway," I say sharply, rising up, wrenching my coat off the chair and throwing it over my back. The chair falls behind me and thuds to the floor on its side, one caster spinning lifelessly.

"Just a minute – we're not done here."

"You're. *You're* not done here. Me? I'm *well* done. Take care, Mitch."

"So, you refuse to answer the questions?" he asks, presumably to present my answer to the judge. He leans toward me as I leave. "You realize that non-compliance with discovery so you can get your nails done is grounds for sanctions and a Motion to Compel?" he threatens.

I tremble theatrically and make sure he sees it. "My nails look better when they're not being deposed." I push the door open in front of me and head out.

"Enjoy your manicure," he offers, dryly, as it closes.

I let him hear my sneer and grunt.

"Idiot." I *don't* let him hear that. I don't want that on the record of course.

But he is one.

I don't care anymore; time for that burger, and a smoke.

That guy tried, but I beat him already.

4: THE DAUGHTER

The Past: ***Tuesday, July 21st 2020***

I love my daughter.

"Hey, baby girl," I ooze.

"How did it go, mama?"

I roll my eyes, but try not to let her see it.

My 12-year-old is lying sideways on the couch against Concepción, her babysitter whom we both love, and they're watching something on Disney+.

Concepción is practically Lela's grandmother at fifty-eight, she's that old, but she's feisty and young in spirit, and we both knew that she'd make for the best person to watch Lela when my shifts at Airway run overtime. She has always loved Lela like a mother.

I should get my nails done, I think to myself. Actually, that's an appointment that Lela never lets me go to by myself. She eats it up. And that's just what we're going to do.

"Oh, man, let's just say that I'm glad it's over. *Long* day," I breathe, ripping off my Covid mask with gusto, as Lela rises and hugs me. I lift up what I was holding behind my back – a bag of oversized chocolate chip cookies someone brought into Airway today. I ate one on the way. Lela squeals with delight and rips the bag out of my hand, returning to the couch to scarf one down.

"Don't you feed my daughter when you're here?" I joke to Concepción with a side-eye. She giggles.

Lela grunts. "Mom, I can make lunch myself. Besides, you said you were bringing these home. Leave Conchita alone."

I chuckle to myself.

Concepción is struggling to get up from the couch. Lela shifts and gives her an arm to steady herself, but it's not enough, so I walk over and help her up. I called her to let her know I was inbound, so she could start preparing. I glance over and her things are behind me by the door. There's a fairly large and transparent tub containing a large assortment of colorful objects under her purse. I hadn't even seen them lying there when I walked in. "It was a long one. *Thank you*, Conchita. Thanks for staying with her so long."

Concepción waves me away. "Oh, uh-huh. It was nothing. Always my pleasure, Tracie. *Mija* knows I love her." Our babysitter winks at my daughter, and Lela runs over and hugs her. Just then I notice that she's wearing some strange new beads around her wrist that match some that Concepción is sporting.

"Oh, look, what are those – are those… new?" I ask, pointing to my daughter's adorned wrist.

"Yeah, mama, aren't they pretty?" Lela holds them up proudly, pivoting her wrist so that I can see every colorful angle.

"Wow! Very nice. Thanks again, Conchita." Never got used to that being a nickname for Concepción. Doesn't seem like it works, but it does.

Concepción holds up her own wrist and shows her own beads, grinning at me. Her puffy black hair has tracing zips of silver through it, and her eyes shine brightly. It's then that I realize what that tub by the door contains. The beads. The ladies made matching bracelets.

"Oh, very nice!" I exclaim. "They *are* pretty!"

"Look, mama, we made one for you," Lela chirps, reaching back onto the end table and fetching one more. "Here, put it on."

I oblige, sliding it over my wrist and letting the thin elastic snap it firmly in place. The beads are translucent, multi-hued, and they grace my arm just like they grace theirs. For a moment the thought runs through me that we all will have to adopt some cutesy girl group name, like we're in a club or something. "Aw, thank you guys. That's sweet."

"Yes, we had fun, didn't we, *mija*?"

Lela turns and nods to Concepción emphatically, a huge grin plastered across her face. They hug.

Concepción turns to hug me as well. "Thank you once more for allowing me time with her!" Her cheek touches mine, and I catch that strong gust – it's not a whiff, it's a *gust* – of *Estée Lauder White Linen*. It's sweet, but it's a bit much. But then again, so is Concepción. She's always been 'much:' *much* love, *much* presence, *much* help, *much* friendliness, *much* sweetness. And she's been so good with Lela for going on four years now, ever since I started working at Airway, transferring over from Kent Regional after that crappy divorce.

Even thinking *about him for a* second...

"You're so welcome, Conchita! Thank *you*, love."

"No problemo. You have to do the hard thing, I'm here for you. You know that."

I nod. She's right. Concepción pulls away and heads for the door, mustering up all her belongings under one shoulder and slinging her old-lady purse over the other. "Adios, amigas! Hasta la próxima!"

Until next time. She always says that.

"See you, Conchita!" Lela says.

The door closes, and it's just the two of us once more. Lela melts into me, and I hold her tightly. She's up to my nose now, having spurted up practically a foot literally overnight. And she's got my muscles too. I wouldn't tangle with her. God be with any boy who tries to. She'll mess them up something awful.

"Sorry I'm late," I whisper into her hair.

"It's okay. I'm sorry it went so long."

"Yeah."

"Why do your days go overtime so much?"

I shake my head and pull away, heading to the kitchen to pour myself some Country Time lemonade. "I don't know, honey. The whole damn schedule is a jo-"

"Aha! That'll be one dollar please."

I roll my eyes. I knew it before I even said it. *The profanity fine.* I haven't even been home for five minutes and she already got me. I dig into my pockets and pull out a flimsy dollar, shaking my head. Good thing I got a cluster of ones a week ago so that I'm ready, at least.

Lela stands there before me, her eyebrows raised, her lips pursed into a thin grin of victory. Her eyes squint triumphantly out at me as she holds her hand out flat and takes my stupid dollar. I slap it into her hand gruffly.

"Well, thank you, ma'am," she utters professionally and then scurries off to her bedroom piggy bank.

"Don't spend it all in one place!" I shout down the hall as I continue to head to the fridge. "Kids and money," I mutter. "God bless 'em both."

Darrell didn't leave me much, the deadbeat jerk. I get DFAS payments and separation payments from my time in the Marines, and I guess Airway pays me okay, but Darrell made plenty of money in Seattle as an investment banker, and, truth be told, we should be in better housing. These apartments are fine, but when I think that he got to keep the house up on the hill, it gets under my skin.

Whatever. That was nine years ago. Lela was barely even three when we split. Thankfully, the animosity turned to contempt, the contempt turned to a separation, and the separation turned to a divorce finalized within only a five-month span, so I didn't have to tolerate any more of his crap. Still: being in the same state as him bugs me, however. He didn't even want custody of Lela. Just wanted to snip ties so he could be with *her*. I grit my teeth. Cheating jerkweed.

Lela jars me out of my memories, practically skipping back into the kitchen, one dollar richer and owning it theatrically. I mock-glare at her, but can't suppress my smile. We stare at each other for a moment, connecting telepathically as only mothers and daughters can. I practically know how her whole day went before she says a word of it. She smiles sheepishly.

"So, it was pretty dumb today? Did you have to process a lot of new guys"

I flick my eyebrows up as I plop down heavily onto my dining table seat. "Yep, as usual. Lots of weirdos out there doing lots of weird things."

"But don't they know you're an ex-Marine and can kick their butts?" she asks, feigning incredulity.

I chuckle, slugging down my Country Time bottle. "They don't care," I finish after a hearty swallow. "Some of the other guards are as well. Semper fi. Doesn't matter. They still got inmates to process, so a girl's gotta do what a girl's gotta do, right? It is what it is."

"Why don't you just show them all your military Judo moves and all that stuff? Then they'd do whatever you say. Right?"

I chuckle. "You watch too many movies," I chide. "I don't know, sweetheart," I answer tiredly, because I am. I'm *tired* after ten hours of work. It couldn't have been any more tolerable even if I had been licked by kittens the entire time. It's the grind. Gotta do the grind. "It's all good, honey," I breathe out. "All good."

"Well, you *did* kinda ask for some hot guys," she says to me with a tilt of her head and a shrug of her shoulders. "See any today?"

I let my lemonade bottle fall from my lips as I stare at her under my eyebrows. "And just whose side are you on, *anyway*?"

Lela giggles. "Yours! Totally yours, mom. You know that. You just said that you get cute guys in there sometimes, and you deserve someone nice, that's all."

I squint my eyes at her. "Your mama deserves a nice convict, does she?"

She shrugs again.

"Yeah, well, I'm sure there are some outside that I could find just as easily."

"Like that guy you met at the store the other day? Bill? You mean *Bill,* mama, the hot guy? *Bill? Billllyyyyyy?* Oh, *Billllllyyy!*" she moans, hugging and rubbing her own shoulders and licking her lips.

"You are *so* gonna get it." I point my Country Time bottle at her. She's unfazed.

"I told you, woman," she says, with a very adult, tired sigh, rising from her seat and practically prancing out into the living room with her soapbox ready to go. "The minute you came home from the store telling me that you thought he was the cutest one yet…"

"I'm gonna beat you," I joke, dryly. "Don't make me come over there."

"Whatever! You're crushing on store randos and cons, and you just can't do that, not with the job you have, girlfriend."

"Oh, it's *girlfriend* now?" I say, staring her down.

"I'm tellin' ya! *You kids.* You just never listen." She shakes her head and turns her back to me. "Oh, *Tracie, Tracie, Tracie,*" she says, clicking her tongue in theatrical disapproval.

"What?!" I cry, pretending to be outraged. It's working. She maintains her act, showing me only her disdain with her face turned away from me. "You little fart!" I yell, and she peers carefully around her head, seeing me sprint toward her.

First there's the shriek… then there's that squeal that I love. And finally, the tremulous running to her bedroom to slam me out and forbid entrance, knowing I'm going to tickle the snot out of her. It's not hard to force my way in.

Continued shrieks and squeals as I push on the door. She still hasn't mastered the whole foot-blocking-the-door technique. Besides, she ain't ex-military. *I* am. My muscles shove that door open, and she retreats to her bed, throwing the covers over herself, as if that were any kind of feasible defense.

In a flash, I'm in and on top of her, jutting solid index fingers everywhere there's flesh still as soft as putty. I especially like to go for her neck, as she emits a series of constrained grunts under the pressure of sensation.

Before a minute's up, I claim victory as we're both panting, and I plop down next to her on her bed, still adorned with her black and pink K-Pop velvet comforter. I still can't remember where I bought it, but I'll never forget her glee when she opened this particular Christmas present.

We're heaving our breaths out in gleeful satisfaction. The pent-up frustration of the day vents upward, and my daughter snuggles up next to me, still giggling. We say nothing; just let the day unwind itself and envelop us in a hearty embrace.

"Hey. Wanna go get our nails done?" I ask her.

She's up and squealing again before I can even say *let's go.* Good. Let's go indeed. We're out to the car and on our way in a flash. They always allow walk-ins.

I just hope I don't see *Bill* again. Lela would never live it up. I shake it off, and before too long, we're sitting side by side, my beautiful daughter and I, and our nails are thanking us.

She loves her mama.

5: THE BROTHER

The Past: ***Thursday, July 23rd 2020***

He's just as cute as his brother.

Gabriel Emory Brickert is the spitting image of his twin, Elias, with all the trappings and tattoos of a chiseled, grizzled, life… just without the incarceration on top of it. When I first set eyes on him, I could swear that he's also either done time, or is about to, because at first glance, he's the one who appears more foreboding and intimidating. He's staunch and strong, but with a strange, quasi-gentlemanly charm.

His face is partially obscured behind his mask, as mine is – as all of ours are, it's mandated, after all – but he's got the same piercing eyes as his brother.

"Greetings, Ms. Vossler. Nice to meet you," he greets me, and extends a warm, meaty hand for me to shake as he sits down in the visitor's office. *Greetings?* Weird way to greet someone. Who says that? Anyway, I don't shake his hand. It's prison policy that we don't touch the visitors or inmates. A virus outbreak in a prison can be deadly, and we're still in the middle of Covid.

"Oh, sorry, we can't. Against the rules."

"Oh, I-" Gabriel flinches suddenly with a curious spasm, his head jerking to the right.

"It's OK, really," I say, waving him off but watching him curiously after that spasm, trying to maintain my composure in the face of such rugged good looks. I honestly don't know which one I'd choose if they were both standing right in front of me right now. "Are you okay? What was that?"

"I'm fine," he says, tiredly. "I have Tourette's."

"Oh, yes, sorry," I say, remembering I saw that on his application. "That was in there. Sorry," I over-apologize to him.

"It's fine. Elias was the lucky one; he didn't get any 'bonuses.'" He smiles self-effacingly. "And as far as Covid goes, I've had all my Moderna shots," he insists, pulling his mask down slightly and grinning as he sits, draping his light cream-colored sports jacket over the back of his chair.

I grin through my mask. “Me too, but you never can tell. Hell, if we were able to shine a light and just see all of the little virus particles floating around all at once, we’d have had this thing licked already.” My eyes are inadvertently drawn downward to his right arm, particularly his bicep. The tattoos are crazy artistic.

Gabriel chuckles. “Licked. Hmmm.”

“Yeah, probably not the right expression with Covid,” I say with a nervous giggle. He’s definitely cute. *Get a hold of yourself, Tracie. What?! He’s not a con,* I argue. *Still – he’s related to one, and you need to pay attention to your job.*

I’ve got his application for visitation open in front of me, and see that he’s the older one – by just under thirty-three minutes. How in the heck their mother was able to maintain her composure and stay conscious during both deliveries that far apart is beyond me.

I motion down to his exposed arms beyond his sleeve. “Those a family custom or something?”

“Huh? Oh, the tattoos? Yeah, Elias has ‘em too, I know. Yeah, I guess you could say so. We got them together in the same salon. We figured, hey, we’re twins, why not get the same thing? Been doing that our whole lives.” It sounds believable, but something in the way he says it says he’s lying. “Anyway, uh, mom always used to dress us up in the same shirts too, ya know? It got old, but those pictures make for a funny stroll down memory lane. Dad didn’t like it too much, he always shook his head and rolled his eyes, but we didn’t mind much, I guess. I can’t really remember.”

That was a mouthful. "Well, it seems like you remember plenty," I say with a proud chuckle. "The good ol' days, right?"

He doesn't answer that question. His eyebrows flick up in a sullen acknowledgment, almost as if he disagrees. I move my eyes back to his application. "It says here you work at Flint Crossing?"

He nods. "Uh, yes. Warehouse Manager."

"Got it. Well, your background report came through clean, and visiting hours open up in seven minutes, so you're good to go."

He flinches again suddenly. I don't want to embarrass him, so I let it go this time. But then, it's strange… my eyes are drawn once more down to his bicep (I can't help it). I find myself staring at it, mesmerized, wondering, and he snaps me out of my fog.

"Ms. Vossler, is something wrong?" he asks, following my stare down to his own bicep. "Do I have something on my shirt?" He tugs at his sleeve, inspecting it.

"No, no, it's fine. Well, uh, Mr. Brickert, you're good to go. I've got you on file, and now you should be able to schedule any further visitations online. I appreciate you coming in, thank you."

"Yeah, yeah, no worries. I'm from here, so it's not like it was a big commute."

"Well, you're also family – *and* his twin – so those are extenuating circumstances that we have to get on file as well. He was only just transferred here from Shelton. New inmates are on probationary process of course."

He snickers. "On probation while serving two life sentences. That's a good one," he mutters, standing.

"Meaning?" I ask, rising with him.

"Oh, nothing. I'm just his only family anymore, and I didn't think he did it. I like to think they got the wrong guy. It's just a lot to… accept," he finishes lamely, his eyes fixed beyond me in a thousand-yard stare.

I smile in sympathy, my eyes flicking back to his bicep once more. Something curious… It couldn't have been. "Oh," I assure him, "just be patient. Sometimes, new evidence comes to light. In the meantime, you're all set to visit him, Elias. *Gabriel!* Sorry. Holy cow, but you guys do look alike."

I can tell he's smiling behind his mask. He waves me away. "Happens all the time. Thanks for your help, Miss…?"

"Vossler."

"That's right, forgot," he says, snapping his fingers and then pointing them at me. "Sorry. Thanks for your help, Officer Vossler. Sorry. It can be a little intimidating in here."

"Understood," I offer, and that's all I offer.

He looks around awkwardly, and that's when I get the clearest sight of his bicep that I've had since the first time. I'm not imagining anything. I'm seeing what I'm seeing. He turns back to me with a curious look of questioning adorning his face.

"Out the door, to the right, all the way down to Deborah on the left, and she can get you set for visitation," I say with a smile.

"Right. Thanks." He starts to leave, opening the door.

"Uh, Mr. Brickert?" I stop him. "Forgetting something?" I'm pointing toward his chair, still draped over by his light cream sports jacket.

"Huh?" he asks, whirling back around. "Oh, yes! Thanks." He gives me a sheepish grin as he re-dons his coat and shakes his head. "I'd lose my cranium if it wasn't glued on straight," he jokes, and then opens the door and starts to head out to the left. I start to say something, but he catches himself, reversing course and starting back to the right instead.

Gabriel Emory Brickert gives me another odd glance as he shakes his head at himself, recriminating. I watch him with my head fixed as only my eyes follow him down the hall through the glass panes of the intake office. I'm part bemused and part curious, bordering on suspicion. This bumbling 'Clark Kent' act he's got – I'm not sure whether it's real or staged. And that leaves me with only one question. Is twin brother Elias Superman, just a bad one?

Either way, they're both… cute but weird.

But it's the weirdness that I can't shake. I know what I saw. When he came in, he had a few strange swirls in his tattoo on his right bicep, with a hollow center. There was nothing there.

And then, when I looked again, it was filled in, with two figures intertwined, holding hands, distinct yet blending formlessly into each other. Two stocky figures, invisible at first, and then revealed, connected. I swear the center of that tattoo was empty before.

Two brothers.

Elias and Gabriel. Gabriel and Elias.

We're all keeping our eyes on the one inside, I think to myself, *but should someone maybe keep their eyes on the one on the outside too?*

He might just be as dangerous as his brother.

6: THE AWKWARDNESS

Present: **Friday, January 8th 2021**

Things are settling down now.

At least in my life they are: the stupid deposition is over, the moron court reporter is out of my hair, and my public defender is going over the transcript. All because this family was involved in what happened. Poor Lela: she had nothing to do with it. She's back in school now, after winter break, and that's a weight off my mind. Also, I can smoke again, although she'd kill me if she found out.

A mob of protesters rushed the capitol building two days ago to protest Joe Biden's election victory. A few even died during the conflict. Crazy stuff. Sometimes it feels like this whole damned world is falling apart, and the weirdest thing is that inside the prison is perhaps, ironically, one of the safest places to be. There's an armory, all the unsafe ones are locked up, and things stay contained. At least, they always used to be that way.

Weird thought, definitely… but true.

I'm out running errands and already grabbed a Wendy's Baconator burger. It doesn't make sense with this body, as they're *so* not good for you… but I couldn't resist. Legal stress makes me crave bacon I think. Anyway, it'll be a few hours until Lela gets home, so she can't get jealous.

Last stop is Safeway for some groceries. Safeway between Ash and Maple is always a good one. For whatever reason the other ones always seem a little rude. This one's out of the way for me and Lela since we live closer to the one off East Mission Avenue, but heck, I'll drive a bit more out of the way for a little old fashioned courtesy.

Railhead Apartments on Sharp have been good to us, and the manager's a sweet old guy who's always quick to fix what I can't. Dad taught me a lot of mechanical know-how growing up with my three older brothers, and I've forgotten a bit of it. So, I give it my best shot, and what I can't fix, Dmitri takes care of it. A good man, that one.

My trusty navy blue Nissan Altima pulls into a stop at Safeway, and before too long, this girl's plopping things into her shopping cart.

It's a beautiful, hot, sunny day, and this summer hasn't spared us any heat. The temperature is eighty-six right now, and Lela and I can't wait to hit the pool tomorrow.

Checkout done, and it's time to head home. Looking forward to some good old-fashioned spaghetti tonight with Lela for our Friday movie night. We started doing that last summer, and it's always been spaghetti. *Over The Moon* is on the playlist for tonight. Never heard of it, but Lela has, and it looks cute.

We'll see. Spaghetti has always been our mutual favorite, with the noodles absolutely drenched in sauce, and the hamburger sprinkled with a heavy dose of Red Robin seasoning. I don't know why, but that's one of the weird bonds we share, and MSG tastes good, so sue us.

I'm halfway out to the parking lot when I see him, and my stomach lurches.

He's standing just behind my car, and both me and my cart jerk to a sudden halt. I just stare at him. It's one thing to see people inside the lockup, but to see them outside and know that they're tied to someone *inside* is just… awkward. But beyond that, there are memories we'll never be able to shake, and I want no part of him. Not anymore. Not after all that has happened.

Keep it together, Tracie. No big deal.

He waves to me, and I can see his gigantic toothy smile devoid of a mask to obscure it, and I'm fighting against being hooked – again. He's frustratingly beautiful – just like his brother was. I wonder if he knows just how attracted I was to Elias. "Greetings, Ms. Vossler!" he says theatrically, once more using that bizarre salutation.

"Gabriel," I breathe. "Uh, *greetings…*"

"Hello, Tracie," he says to me. I look around to see if anyone is watching. A light breeze wafts through his locks, sending them skyward for a brief moment – they're the same as his brother's – and I force a smile. "Good to see you. I saw you pull in."

"Oh? How nice," I say, my mechanical smile stretching across my plastic cheeks as I dutifully open my trunk and place things inside. "Have you been waiting long?"

He moves over to the side of my car and watches me, his hands in his pockets. "No, no, just got here. You had the same idea I did. Spaghetti, huh?"

"Friday night special," is all I can say. I don't want to be nice to him, I don't want to talk to him, but I'm caught between awkwardness and obligation.

"Great. Sounds delicious. When should I be over?"

I turn to him with a slight jerk, and my expression signals my incredulity. He scoffs.

"I'm kidding, I'm kidding. I can make my own. Do you take your spaghetti with or without crushed Skittles in it?" His eyebrows flick up and his mouth remains in a crap-eating grin.

I'm speechless for a second, but I have to answer him and draw the line. My eyes are inadvertently drawn to his right bicep again, trying to see through his T-Shirt. For a moment I'm not sure if I'm wanting to investigate that strange tattoo, or merely enjoying his muscles once more. I'm hoping for the former, but guessing the latter. I know myself too well.

I have to shake myself out of the fog. I know what happened, and he's still freaky, no matter how much – or little – time has passed. I'm not over it. And he shouldn't be here!

"Look, Gabriel," I start, hesitantly, "I promised I wouldn't talk to you, and I want nothing to do with any of what happened. Not anymore."

He nods quickly. "Oh, I completely understand," he says, with a grimace, and there's disappointment there. "I get it. It's fine." Gabriel takes a gargantuan breath, and his chest thrusts upward. He holds it in for an intolerable minute. "Still so hard to talk about, ya know? Losing Elias. You're like the one thread that I still have to him is all it is." I swallow hard, trying to read through his words. "Hard to," -here he pauses and his eyes fall to the ground- "let go, that's all."

I nod. "Mm-hmmm. Okay. I just – with everything that happened, they're looking to the people who saw what went down, and I was part of that. You know that, Gabriel." I grimace.

"Hard to believe they keep hounding you. I mean, you, your daughter, you should be free of all of this by now," he attempts to empathize.

I don't answer. I don't want to.

We stare at each other for an awkward moment, wondering who will win the silence contest. An elderly woman with a fully loaded cart struggles by us with a wink and a smile. I clench my lips into an obligatory beam for her.

When my eyes return to Gabriel, he's staring right into my soul. It's unnerving. I feel completely nude. There's something in his eyes, and his visage has changed somewhat, like there's the trace of a grin underneath the heat of that stare…

"You loved him, and now, it's hard to look at me because you see Elias."

That's all he says, and it's enough. I inadvertently roll my eyes and let my head loll around as I get back to unloading my cart. I give him my back, but not out of contempt. I'm trying to be nice; I just need to get going. The goosebumps are rising on my neck and arms.

"Gabriel, no, that's not it, I-" I turn back to my cart, but I wince as if I've been stabbed. "I mean, *yes*, of course, I do see him in you, but…" -here I'm talking faster and faster in my nervousness as I thrust things frustratedly into the trunk of my Altima- "that's not the reason. I mean, the reason is…. I just- ok, I don't *know* the reason, okay? All I know is that I'm under pressure to put this whole thing behind me. Behind us-"

I turn to where Gabriel was. The void left by his departure is palpable.

Gabriel is nowhere to be found. My head wildly rotates all around, my eyes searching desperately. I didn't even feel the wind of his departure. He's gone, leaving his accusation suspended heavily in the air over me.

I swallow roughly, glancing around everywhere and not finding him. My goosebumps are at maximum height, and a chill runs down my spine.

All I can do is grunt, continuing to balance slowly placing the groceries in the trunk while scanning the parking lot for any trace of him. There's a weird, faint smell of sulfur in the air suddenly, and it makes me queasy. My stomach begins to revolt once more. That Wendy's burger feels like it's on its way back up.

All I want to do is get home. Elias was cute but weird… but Gabriel is weird but cute, and I'm finding myself wishing Elias was still here, when, in reality, I shouldn't be wishing for either of them.

The smell of sulfur lingers. I can't stay here anymore.

I return my cart to the cart corral, and it happens to be right by where the old lady is parked. She notices me instantly, and turns, as she's still unloading. "Need some help?" I offer, meekly.

"Oh, thank you, yes, darling!" she exults. "Milk is *heavy*!" She frowns.

"Don't I know it."

"Your friend was quite the dish," she offers in a sweet maternal tone, and for a moment I'm reminded of Concepción, just without the accent or the *Estée Lauder*. I look blankly at her. "Did you get his number?"

I grunt, but save the eyerolling for later. "Not really my type," I finish, with a shake of the head. *If you only knew, lady…* I think.

"What? Well, if you don't take him, I *will,* sweetie!" Her eyebrows tease upward and she cocks her head to the side in a sly smile with pursed lips. It's all I can do to suppress a guffaw.

"You win," I say, and she giggles, as I help her load her things into her car. She thanks me, and I'm back to my car to head for home. One last scan of the parking lots reveals no

Gabriel, but I have no idea which car might be his. It's creepy and unnerving.

That old lady doesn't even know what she's wanting. I had no idea, myself.

I'm looking forward to spaghetti with Lela tonight. With that creepazoid here, I wasn't sure I could stomach even the thought of it.

But my tummy is settling now.

7: THE CRYPTIC

The Past: ***Sunday, August 2nd 2020***

They're doing what everyone does.

First one raises their hand up against the glass, and then the other raises theirs, and they press first their fingertips and then their palms together in parallel through a thin windowpane.

They nod to each other. The pane is there to separate them from touching each other, but that doesn't stop them from connecting. None of them.

It certainly isn't stopping Gabriel and Elias now.

Communications are all monitored in non-contact visits, and their visitation phones may seem private in their individual kiosks, but they all go through security where they're being monitored, and will be evaluated later for any cryptic messages or hidden meanings.

Gabriel has removed his mask, and Elias as well. We let them remove them for these visits; they're not actually 'visits' in the strictest sense of the word anyway. Not at least where Covid could be exchanged through that glass.

I love being on rotation; that's the one thing about Airway that I appreciate. Some correctional institutions have designated positions that you're plunked down into and that's it; that's all she wrote. That's where you serve, period. Cathcart is in Admissions, and that's the only place he is. But they offered me a 'rover' position when I first started – there are several of us like that – to allow for some flexibility in where we serve, so that if one area becomes a bit more difficult or mundane, we have the option to switch. I prefer it that way, because it lends itself to a little variety.

Or perhaps, I prefer it that way because now I can keep my eyes on both Brickert brothers. That bizarre tattoo shift hasn't left me, and I'm curious what else is going to happen with this Gabriel dude now that he's visiting. His first visit went well, or so the report says. We'll see what happens on this one. I'm listening intently.

Gabriel: *Hey brother.*

Elias: *Hey, good to see you. Thanks for coming.*

Gabriel: *Of course. You doin' okay?*

Elias: *Yeah, I guess. Not too bad.*

Gabriel: *You up on your meds? You can't slip on those, ya know. Don't want any more episodes, right?* There's the faint trace of a smirk as Gabriel says that.

Elias: *No! No more episodes. Man! I never want another episode.* I can see Elias shaking his head, and my heart goes out to him in pity.

Gabriel: *I hear you. How's the chow?*

Elias: *Same as always. You know, shit on a shingle. The commissary we get to order is better. Chi Chi always hits the spot. Hook-up ain't bad either. Basically, anything with Ramen in it.* Elias chuckles.

Gabriel: *Always hated the shrimp flavor.*

Elias: *Yeah, me too.*

Gabriel: *Makin' any friends?*

Elias sneers: *You don't make* friends *in here, bro.*

Gabriel: *No, I suppose not. Right.*

Elias pauses: *Anyway...* He sniffs. *So, did you do it?*

At this, my eyes squint, and I listen more intently. I can see the twins on the monitor in front of me, split-screen. It's grainy, but I can make out Gabriel's slow spread of a smile across his face.

Gabriel: *I did, bro. You don't feel it?*

Elias: *Nope.*

Gabriel: *You will. Mom would be proud.*

Elias: *She would, huh?*

Gabriel: *Oh yeah. She definitely would. Dad would be too.*

Elias: *You… you sure you got it right? I mean, you can't mess that kind of stuff up, bro.*

Gabriel: *I know! Seriously. Yes. I paid attention.*

Elias: *So… when does it kick in?*

Gabriel: *Soon. You'll know. Trust me.*

Elias: *OK.* He takes a deep breath. *OK,* he says again.

Gabriel: *Just relax, little brother.* Just then, he flinches. The same weird spasm as before. It's brief, but I catch it.

Elias sneers again: *Give me a break with that. Thirty-three minutes isn't like you were in the army when I was in middle school, butthead.*

Gabriel chuckles. *I know, I know. Sorry.*

Elias: *Well, I'm looking forward to… it. Thanks, bro.*

Gabriel chuckles. *Of course. It'll happen. Just be patient, brother.* Then, as if sensing that what they've been discussing might be decoded in real-time, he throws a diversionary bone. *The lawyers will get you out of here, I promise.* An almost imperceptible wink from Gabriel here. *Just wait. I promise.*

Elias: *Sounds good, bro. What else is happenin' on the outs?*

Gabriel chuckles. *Oh, the same ol' same 'ol. Sickness running rampant through society. People are afraid. Same as in here, right?*

Elias: *Same as in here. Sure enough.*

Gabriel: *Covid's got everyone up in arms. People are slowly tiring of the masks, I think. I know I am.* Here he tugs at his mask and pretends to rip it off and chuck it into the distance.

Elias snickers. *They're spraying down their mail, for goodness' sake. No one is getting married, having public gatherings, churches are closed. Stuff like that. I love it.*

Elias: *Well, it'll be good to be out again, that's for sure.*

My eyes squint again. Elias Brickert is in here for two consecutive life sentences. He's already been in and out of court, and the gavel slammed down. He's not getting out of here. He was in jail, then Shelton, then Airway Heights. He's in the system now and not going anywhere. Something's up. I don't care how cute they are. I'm not wasting any more time. There's definitely something fishy going on here, and their cryptic communication is bleeding red with suspicion.

I hit the intercom. "Brickert, 9254381, visit is over, repeat visit is over. Visitor, please exit to the lobby."

Both twins glance up in surprise at the overhead intercom, and then emit a sullen, dejected chuckle with a grim smile on both of their mugs as they look at each other. Once more they press their hands to the glass. Once more, they nod. And that's it.

But not before Gabriel spasms. Something fishy about that one. Tourette's or no Tourette's, that whole exchange was a bit too arcane for my taste, and I've got to report it.

Their fingers separate, and Elias hangs up. Gabriel hangs up his phone and stands, retreating to the lobby. Forrester, a guard who I only know by name, lets him out to the lobby. Time to tattletale.

2:17pm

"You're sure that's what he said?"

Superintendent Caleb Canton is a good warden. A decent man, also ex-military, but he was in the Army. Some kind of computer mumbo-jumbo position, tech stuff. Beyond me. 64 and graying, he's a thick husk of a man that you would *not* want to tangle with, but there's a cool administrative side to him that belies his tanklike appearance. He's got a good head on his shoulders. His tiny, dark office isn't big enough for it or him.

"Absolutely. It's right there in the footage."

"Well, that's the weird part, though, isn't it?"

"What?" I ask. "I don't follow."

"Well, it's being cleaned up by Jensen to see what else he can find, but every time they're saying what you said they're saying, all that stuff about getting out and… whatever it was about their mom and dad, and all that… you can't hear it."

My jaw drops, and boy do I frown. "What? What do you mean, you can't hear it? Are you kidding? I heard it plain as day in monitoring."

"Well, I don't know what you heard in real-time, but I'm not hearing any of that stuff here." Canton turns his monitor toward me to play back the visitation footage. I can see their lips moving, but it's like the audio is distorted… or gone. All I hear is white noise.

"That's- not possible," I utter, slowly.

"Well, possible or not, there it is. I'll let you know what Jensen says when he reports back."

"But you can see their lips moving, right, Caleb? Tell me I'm not crazy. Look!" I point to the screen, just as the footage plays back the section where the Brickert twins are discussing how Elias will get out of there. "See?"

"I do see their lips moving, but I don't know why we're not hearing anything," he replies gruffly. "That's why I sent it to Jensen. That's all I can say. But I've noted down what you said they discussed. Was there any talk of, uh, I don't know, 'dates' or- or did they mention a timeline for when you said they talked about Brickert 'getting out'?"

"No, no- nothing like that. I'm stumped." I'm still staring at the screen, incredulous.

"Well, if you had good reason to terminate a visit, then so be it. I trust you, Tracie. Just keep your eyes on them. I know Forrester took Elias back to his cell. You said you had a talk with his brother after that, out in the lobby?"

"Yessir. I split them up and then went out and talked with him. It's like he was playing dumb or something. Like he couldn't remember them even discussing it."

Canton just stares at me, presumably about as confused as I am.

"I'm serious. No recollection. I mean, I've met some pretty good liars in my lifetime, but I honestly almost believed him. It genuinely seemed he didn't remember it."

Canton sighs. "Alright. We'll bring Elias in for questioning," he says, and then he reaches back to an intercom phone behind him. He taps *R Building*. "Warden Canton. I need Brickert, 9254381, to Central, please." I hear the dim voice respond something staticky on the other end. "Thank you."

The superintendent hangs up and slowly turns back to me. "Alright. Let's hear what we didn't hear."

I frown, awaiting the inevitable.

2:33pm

Elias Brickert sits now before Superintendent Canton, and from all outward appearances, he's confused too.

"I honestly don't know what you're saying," he defends. "We didn't talk about my parents."

"So, what you're saying," Canton shoots back, pointing at me, "is that Officer Vossler here is lying. Is that right?"

Brickert deflates, and grunts. "That's not what I'm saying at all, Warden, Officer Vossler. I'm serious. I'm not saying that. I just don't know what you heard."

My heart goes out to him for a moment, because he genuinely seems oblivious to the charges leveled at him right now, and it doesn't seem like Canton is going to let him off easy. He's gunning for him, and he believes me.

"What I heard was you and your brother talking about some kind of deliverance from prison that sounded like it was on the way, and something about your parents being proud of you. You don't remember any of that?"

"No, I don't!" he says forcefully, throwing his hands up momentarily. "And the reason I say that is because we intentionally *don't* talk about our parents. We don't like to."

"Why?" Canton asks.

Elias sighs. "It's a long story. It's just background noise now, but we didn't have the best upbringing, okay? I don't wanna talk about this."

"Why not?" Canton prods again, rising from his seat and placing himself on the corner of his desk uncomfortably close to Elias, invading his space bubble. I can't tell if it's intentional or not. Maybe it is. Maybe that's how he works and gets what he wants out of the guys here.

"Because it stirs up things in me that I don't want to feel anymore," he says, helplessly. "Things that Gabriel doesn't want to feel either."

Canton and Elias stare at each other. I'm not entirely sure the superintendent is convinced, but Elias is doing a great job telling him why he didn't say what I heard him say. I don't get it. I'm watching him, and it's either the best acting job I've ever seen, or he truly believes in what he's telling us. Give this guy an Oscar, or give him sanctions. What to do?

"Brickert, this is your last chance. Either 'fess up, or you're going to go in the hole for the night while we continue to investigate. We've got a technician working on it and he'll be glad to- well, actually, look here, I just got his message." Canton checks his message, reading through it: presumably a reply from Jensen. He scowls.

"You're going to send me to the hole for something I didn't even do?" Elias barks back. His jawline is as fierce as an etched rock, and it's clear he feels this is incredibly unjust.

"Because of something that Officer Vossler here *thinks* she heard? No offense," he says to me.

I shrug my shoulders.

Canton again says nothing, just puts his phone down and stays on the corner of his desk with his arms crossed, watching Brickert while he sits there in the superintendent's crosshairs. Elias is stone-faced except for the bristling incredulity under his brow. A smoldering line could be drawn from eye to eye: Canton's glaring orbs and Elias', well, *cute* ones.

Canton relents first, but not in the defeated sense. He rises, uncrosses his arms, and calls upon Titus, the guard just outside his office. Titus enters. "Stand up and turn around please, Mr. Brickert."

Brickert sighs heavily and rolls his eyes as he stands. "You're making a mistake," he grimaces.

"What was that?" Canton says sharply, gripping Brickert by the shoulders as Titus stops cuffing him momentarily. He glares at the inmate.

Elias doesn't repeat himself. I think he realizes he slipped, and it's better that he bites his tongue. He just resorts to staring forward stoically, his lips pursed. Canton then goes in for the kill.

"It's that kind of attitude that got you in here, inmate. If I were you, I'd stow any further lip, because you'll just extend your stay at Hotel Hole. Got it?"

No answer from Elias.

Officer Titus circles around to his rear and escorts Elias Brickert out of the superintendent's office. As Elias is led out, the two of us remain, watching his departure. Just before Elias rounds the corner, there's one, brief, slow glance my way.

And in that glance, there's either sorrow – or pity.

I can't tell if its sorrow is for his own predicament, or pity as a direct continuation of the threat that he had basically made on the superintendent.

Verbiage is important around here. You have to watch what you say if you're an inmate at Airway. It's not Alcatraz, but it's not a water park either. An indictment of the superintendent's actions constitutes a potential threat against him, and that's the way it has to be treated. Elias sat through orientation and he was briefed on the rules.

So, if that look is remorse for having to spend a day – or even a few days – in the hole while Jensen parses out that recording, *tough luck, man.* That's the rules of Airway. But if it's pity on us as some kind of credible attitude of threat, then I bet Canton noticed it, and he'll take preventative measures. Maybe by keeping him in the hole for an extended duration.

Either way, Elias is cooked for now.

"That went well," I lament, turning back to Canton and sitting back down in my chair across from him. He flicks his eyebrows up at me but keeps his arms crossed. "What now?"

He shrugs. "He enjoys a little time away from society until he can learn to play by the rules like everyone else here does."

"Not everyone," I grunt with a roll of my eyes.

"Well, if he wants to be part of that demographic, that's his problem. Model citizens don't last long in the joint, but we appreciate them while they do," Canton says, rubbing his face with a yawn as he, too, sits. We eye each other for a moment. "Well, I better get back to visitation, that's where I'm at for today and I don't know how much longer Flansburg is covering for me in there. That okay?" Canton *hmmms* a 'yes' my way, returning to his screen. I'm almost out the door and back to visitation.

"Just keep an eye on that guy," he says to me. "Jensen wrote back. There was *nothing* in the recording. So, either he – or *you* – aren't exactly being upfront with me. You I trust. I only trust him as far as I could throw him."

I don't know what to say, honestly. I stand there gobsmacked… not sure if it's more from the fact that the presumption of innocence has effectively been suspended for me, while the continuing presumption of guilt of all the inmates here goes on unabated. I just look at him, fazed.

"Get what they say correct. Every time. I don't have time for these hairbrained he-said she-said. I need it on tape."

I nod. There's nothing I can do it about it not being on tape. Nothing. Jensen doesn't find anything, there's nothing I can do, but I know what they said and I know what I heard.

"Yes sir, Superintendent," I acknowledge quietly, and head back out to visitation, more confused than ever. But I can't stop shaking my head the entire way back.

August 3rd, 2020, 12:09am

The witching hour. I hate this time of day, and this shift has gone *way* too long already. I'm tired, and I'm not off until one. Thank God for Concepción. God bless that lady, indeed.

Lela's got to get up for school in only six short hours, and I'm going to be a freaking zombie when she does. Thankfully she can make her own breakfast. I touched base with Concepción in the early evening, and video chatted with Lela on my smoke break before she went to bed, so that's all well and good, but I'd much rather be home, all things considered.

I'm sure Elias hates me. I wonder what Gabriel is thinking out there. Even after I talked with him, it didn't clear the air, and I felt something was still weird about the whole thing. Just 'off.' I wonder if Caleb will bring him in for some sort of continuing investigation. There's been nothing new from Jensen, and I don't suppose there will be.

Whatever.

I take another long drag on my smoke and put it out. Right as I snuff it into the tray, the siren goes off. The lights go up all over the prison yard. Training kicks in and I'm running back inside to central to see what's up. Someone is yelling something over the intercom and I can't hear it. I think it's Cathcart.

There's a chatter of guards' voices all around me as we mobilize. Some of them I know. Someone reported an inmate got iced. Another says it was a *hot one*, which means the same thing, but sounds completely different in temperature. Either way, someone just got their life snuffed out of them.

We gang together and head out, a small security force, to meet the guard on duty. A few of us are brandishing capture shields. A few have batons. I do.

Squawking voices come over the radios. The murder was in the R Building. McFarland is the chief out there. That's where Elias was before he was sent to the hole. I briefly wonder how he's doing in there. McFarland had talked with Elias here and there – the guards do that: they treat them civilly – but he's had no contact with him since he's been in the hole of course.

The air is hot and stuffy outside. The sun set hours ago, but the lingering broil remains settled over the prison yard, and we trudge through it.

In a moment, we're in R Building, and there's a babel and clatter of people talking over each other. All of the inmates in Medium Custody here are in their cells with the doors locked. Many are awake, and peeking out of their cell door windows.

McFarland takes point. He's calling the guards with him. We head upstairs, flanking each other, the shields in front. He leads us down the second level catwalk against the parapet, with a small lane of travel down to the cell in question. The lights are blindingly bright here in the R Building well after midnight.

McFarland leads us on. My knuckles tighten around my baton, wielded below my waist.

"Right here. R-41," says a guard coming toward us. There's another one stationed outside the cell in question. I don't know whose it is.

"He ain't movin!" says the other guard.

The guard closest to us motions us forward. McFarland barks at the onlooking inmates, perched at their doors and awaiting further word on the entertainment value they're experiencing right now in the thick of night. Everyone's curious who got whacked.

"Right here," says the guard with McFarland. "In here. Dead as a doorknob," he finishes, and then solemnly exhales sadly. "That is *no* way for a man to die."

As we round the corner, I can see two other guards bobbing in and out of the cell, and they've got an inmate pinned up against the wall. He's shouting something unintelligible to them.

We're almost there.

Man, I'm tired. *Man,* I wish I was just home with Lela. It's anxiety peaks like this that make me wish I worked at Starbucks instead. I grip my baton even tighter.

The guard utters quietly, "looks like he's been dead for about an hour now. Just before the turn of the clock."

We're at the cell door. The two guards have the murderer in their custody, and he's cuffed. His back is turned to us. And that's when my eyes are drawn to something that no one should ever have to see.

R-41 is splattered with blood. It's everywhere. The walls are dripping. The murderer's cellie appears to be standing – at least at first glance.

The victim's hands have unceremoniously been tied to the top posts of their bunk, fanning outward as if crucified. His face is a mass of blood, and, peering in, I can see his own tongue has been sewn into his eyes – seemingly while he was still alive. It's split right down the middle, separating at the base of his tongue inside his mouth. Scarlet swaths river down his neck, and his face and shoulders – and the rest of him, really – are dotted with blood. His eyebrows are a downward mash of discontent and surprise.

He is naked, suspended, hanging from the bedposts with a material I don't recognize. Rivulets of blood run from his wrists. In that position is where he took his last heaving breaths. I don't know how quickly his cellie turned on him – or why – but he did his job of finishing the victim off with a macabre finesse.

"Yep, that's McAllister," one of the guards. "Dude's dead."

McAllister. Why does that name sound familiar?

My eyes widen. That was Elias Brickert's cellie.

The guards rotate the surviving inmate to face us. He is clothed and battered with blood spew, but I recognize those eyes and that lanky hair.

Elias Brickert.

But that's not possible – he was in the hole, in isolation from the general population. *What?* How could he be here? They walk him toward and past me. As they do so, Elias turns to me with a smirk, and utters three words that demolish my grasp of the moment:

Greetings, Ms. Vossler.

My brows both furrow in confusion, and my mouth drops open. But… Gabriel was the one who said that. Not Elias. *Gabriel…*

My body turns involuntarily as I follow him out with my eyes. They lead him back down the walkway as other inmates shout catcalls through their cells, watching with great interest and relish.

My eyes don't leave Elias Brickert.

Elias Brickert who just used Gabriel Brickert's weird salutation on me. A chill runs through me.

What is this?

What's going on?

And why was Trenton McAllister just killed by this new inmate, in such gruesome fashion?

He did exactly what his brother did…

PART TWO: THE TRADE

8: THE GRAVITY

The Past: ***Tuesday, August 4th 2020***

I know now.

I still don't get it, however, and I'm still thoroughly confused as to what happened. How could it be? It *can't* be. There's just no way.

Elias Brickert killed Trenton McAllister.

In the wake of the murder, Gabriel Brickert was brought in and then released on his own recognizance after initial questioning. They can't pin anything to him because, first of all, it wasn't physically possible for it to *be* him, and all evidence was purely circumstantial; he would have walked out of that courtroom laughing at the impudence and audacity of it all. And the fingerprint test they gave him didn't have enough differentiation in the swirls between he and his brother for them to conclusively single *either* out as the perp. That alone was cause for concern, so now both of them have a file opened with the FBI.

As for Elias, I was there when they questioned him. And that explanation could get him committed. I could hardly believe it when I heard it. Elias stated that Gabriel was simply trying to help him. Gabriel had performed a 'forbidden ritual' from their dead mother's occult journals, Elias said. It had backfired, he said. The two of them were tied at birth, but Gabriel was trying to 'tie them together further in life.'

But something happened. There's *someone else* in the picture now, he said, and that just creeps me out. Who, exactly, he wouldn't say, but the hairs on my neck stood up when he said it. All Elias would say is "Gabriel opened the door again. He's back."

Honestly, I'm not sure I believe in that kind of occult crap. Canton doesn't believe in it, certainly, so Elias was barking up the wrong tree with him, with the police, with the investigators, with everybody.

Elias wasn't speaking clearly as they were cleaning him. He kept saying *He's in here, he's in here, he's in here. Once more, just like last time, he's in here,* he'd say. It was utterly bizarre! *Who* is in *where*, we asked him. No response.

But it was Gabriel, sure enough, plain as day, who got escorted out of Elias Brickert's cell. How, I still don't know, but it had to be. It *had* to be. That was *not* Elias.

The very next day, however, that was Elias that I talked to in further questioning about the event. They brought him out of the hole, and since I was the one who processed him into Airway and also had contact with Gabriel, the FBI deposed me informally in tandem with Elias' session. Neither the Feds nor the state police believed his story, nor mine about what I had heard the brothers say in the visitation.

To them, it was cut and dry: Gabriel Brickert was a free citizen, innocent, on the outside, and that was none other than Elias Brickert in there: bloodied, post-murder, having barbarically killed his cellie, Trenton McAllister. Elias is back in the hole once more, with the guard doubled. And that's another matter entirely: no one can explain how he got out of solitary and back into his own cell in the first place.

If they weren't identical twins, and *utterly* identical to the nth degree at that – even down to the very fingerprints – this would be a slam dunk. But it isn't.

None of it makes sense, and I've got to get to the bottom of it. Canton rode me pretty hard about what I said I heard them say in their visit, and I need to prove to him that it was true, because it has bearings on the murder.

So, against Airway policy, I contacted Gabriel privately and asked him to meet with me.

I eventually filed my report, got off shift and went home. I *finally* got some sleep, though it was fitful. Woke up, showered, and was on my way to Flint Crossing warehouse. I would have accosted Gabriel there had he declined, but thankfully he agreed to meet with me.

His story was too bizarre. It's still too bizarre.

And he's still a free man. Should he be?

Gabriel Brickert committed murder. He had to have done it. Not Elias. But Elias has yet to corroborate Gabriel's story; to confirm or deny anything. There's nothing I can do about it until then. They didn't believe me then, and they don't believe me now.

I've got to *make* them believe me.

"It's not possible, Gabriel. It's just not."

Gabriel just stares at me, stone-faced. He says nothing. There's something about his eyes as he watches me. Almost like they belong to someone else. The body is Gabriel's: free, debonair, muscular, and intimidating. The external appearance says it's Gabriel, but the demeanor within *feels* like another person entirely – perhaps even Elias. It feels gentler than Gabriel. I almost want to believe him.

"Can you please *say* something?" He doesn't. "An inmate was just *murdered*, Gabriel – in your *brother's* cell. And the crazy thing is that Elias wasn't even supposed to be there. He was in the hole! Explain that to me." He doesn't.

I'm tired of this. I let loose a beleaguered sigh and a profane grunt, throwing my hands up and turning away from him. "You know, I should have expected nothing less from you. You're creepy as hell, you and your brother have some weird occult thing going on, and the prison is looking to *me* because they think I knew something was going to happen from your conversation in the visit. I can't go to them with *occult* crap, Gabriel. Throw me a freaking bone here, *please!*"

A silence falls between us. A murder of crows caws suddenly and incessantly in the distance, chasing away an eagle that dared to veer too close to them. In the midst of that, a voice suddenly, quietly, speaks, low and enchanting.

"Ms. Vossler, have you ever heard of Bodhayana's *Bhagavadajjukam*?"

"What?" I ask in irritation, whirling back around to him. Gabriel is staring at me with piercing eyes that drill into my sense of ease under deep brows that act as a blanket for the spirit within. A frown wraps his face.

He continues.

"It's an ancient Hindu yogic and spiritual tradition found in old Vedic and Sanskrit writings. It was practiced by yogis, did you know that?" he asks, and then his eyes fall to the ground as if lost in thought, while a smile wrapped in memory stretches one side of his lips upward.

"Never heard of it," I breathe skeptically.

"Not many have," he instantly acquiesces. "It's kind of a lost art. Parakaya pravesha. It's a siddhi, a supernatural yogic power that lets a practitioner leave their body and enter another."

Now I'm creeped out even more. I continue to watch him, waiting for any of this to make sense.

"It's not practiced much anymore, but Indian thinking has been deeply invested in the idea of mind-body dualism for more than a thousand years, though the ideas predate that. In *Bhagavadajjukam,* a yogi with siddhi powers, along with his student, meet an Ajukka who dies from a snakebite. A messenger from Yama, the deity of death, takes her soul. The disciple convinces the guru to employ parakaya pravesha to bring her body back to life. The guru's soul goes into the Ajukka's body, bringing it back to life with his personality and wisdom. The Ajukka's soul goes into the guru's empty body. The Ajukka now acts like a holy ascetic, quoting scriptures, and the guru acts like a sexy Ajukka, dancing and flirting." He snickers as he tells me the story. "It's actually quite comical."

"I don't think any of this is comical, Gabriel."

His eyes return to mine with an uncanny stare, and I can't help but see Elias in that gaze once more.

"Our mother was Hindu, Ms. Vossler. She was obsessed with it. Our father never liked it, but that didn't stop her. She even changed her name to a Hindu name."

"What was her name?" I ask, growing more curious.

"Julia," he says, gently, and there's a trace of an endearing smile there, remembering his mother. "She changed it to Aadhya. It means *first power.*"

"Is that a fact?" I ask nonchalantly, but I'm no longer curious, seeing where he's going with this.

"Yes," he says, grimly, and I notice a sparkle in the corner of his eye. His memory turns to grief.

"She *was* a power, Ms. Vossler. And when that change occurred, Julia ceased to exist. It was only Aadhya from that point forward. Our father," -here he pauses, gritting his teeth-

"well, she was no longer the woman he married, and that does change the dynamic, doesn't it?"

I clench my own lips, thinking back to my ex, Darrell. He had definitely changed. He became someone utterly different from the man I married.

"In that exchange, she outgrew him," he says. "She became powerful. She could… *do things*. *Unique* things. Some might call them *dangerous* things."

"Can you get to the point, please? I'm aging," I whine to him, and he chuckles through his nose, subtly.

"I'm getting there, I promise." He takes a deep breath, and his face is awash with concern and resentment. "We were born three years later. Identical twins."

"Yeah, I got that part."

"Mother kept a journal. All of her writings, all of her rituals, everything that made Aadhya *Aadhya*. By that time, they were divorced. Mother was growing increasingly bizarre and kept up her incantations to a maddening degree. That's when our father died. The day he died she-"

He stops, cold. His lips move noiselessly for a while, and I squint my eyes to hear what he's saying, if anything.

"What, Gabriel? She what?"

"The carnival."

I frown.

"She took us to a carnival that very day," he utters, staring off into the silent distance. "We didn't know he died; we found out about it later. In the carnival, we went to one of those mirror mazes, do you know the ones?" I nod. "No one else was in there. It was a weekday, and the carnival was not open to the public yet. She snuck us in through the fence," he says as he emits a self-effacing chuckle. "Aadhya – cut our palms. She had us clasp hands while having us chant in some strange language. We didn't know what we were saying, we were so young. I still don't know what it was. But *he* knew."

I'm slowly approaching him as slowly as he approaches his point – if there even is one – with equally slow relish. "*Who* knew, Gabriel? *Who* knew *what*?"

His eyes rise to meet mine, and I see that same look of regret that he gave Canton and I as he was escorted to the hole. "*Moloch* knew."

"Okay, I give up. Who's Moloch?" I prod.

"He's a spirit, Tracie. A very powerful spirit. Someone Aadhya ushered in accidentally during her incantations. You must understand she wasn't a trained shaman. Aadhya had powers, and she knew the spells, but she didn't know how to safeguard herself – *or us.* That's when Moloch met her and entered our life, before he – ultimately killed her." He stops, as if searching his memory. "I don't know how. It possessed me and my brother. It took on the ambience of the hall of mirrors, and it could 'ride' either of us, mirrored twins, at will. We were only eight."

"You've *got* to be kidding me," I jab, unwilling to believe this paranormal mumbo-jumbo he's slopping. "I don't believe in any of that crap."

"I'm not kidding you. I'm telling you the truth. There are secrets in our family history he has exploited, and will continue to exploit."

"Gabriel, just *stop* it, okay? Enough."

And that's when he drops the bomb on me.

"Tracie, my name is not Gabriel – Emory – Brickert. And I think you already sense that," he says, defiantly. "My name is Elias – James – Brickert. I swear this to you on my father's grave."

"You expect me to believe this, *Gabriel*?" I ask him, deliberately emphasizing his name. "Come on."

"You sense it. Don't lie," he says, sternly. "You can tell that I'm Elias. Of course, I look like Gabriel. We are twins, after all. But it's me, Ms. Vossler. Elias. And that's Gabriel in there, right now, in the hole."

"Right," I say, with my arms now crossed.

"I'm telling you the truth," he insists. "Moloch left us alone for many years, but he's back. Gabriel- he tried to perform one of mother's spells that would give me a reprieve. He cares for me. He wanted to provide a break or... a breath of fresh air. He wanted to release me for a time, so that he could bear my suffering and I could be free. He had to try."

"And so – what? He freed you and took your place and *he* killed McAllister?"

"*Neither* of us killed him, Ms. Vossler. *Moloch* killed him. Moloch is loose now, and Gabriel- he let him in," he says, mournfully.

"Right," I say again. "But if that's the truth, *Elias,* then your ass is supposed to be back in prison. You're guilty of murder already. That's the whole reason you were in prison in the first place, and you should be back there. You can't just go gallivanting around the countryside just because your brother wants you to." I shake my head and roll my eyes at the cartoonish idiocy of what I just said. I have to admit, there's a gravity to what he's saying, and if it's even remotely true, then it's got to be the weightiest and most outlandish thing I've ever heard. Either that or he's telling me the greatest lie I've ever heard: one that would rival the tall tales that Lela used to tell as a little girl.

"You heard our conversation yourself a few days ago in visitation-"

"Yeah. The conversation which you denied right afterward, which places me on the chopping block."

"That was not our intention."

"*Our* intention? Who, you, Elias, and this… this freaky *Moloch* dude?" I sneer with a contemptuous laugh.

His sternness continues. "It's not a laughing matter. You should *not* be joking about this, Tracie."

"Hey. It's Ms. *Vossler* to you, alright? And I have half a mind to get our legal counsel on this so they can get a judge to issue a warrant for your arrest, Gabriel."

"I'm *Elias*. And you know it in your heart. Because of what Gabriel said to you after you saw the body."

Greetings, Ms. Vossler.

I swallow hard as I remember.

"Bullshit. So, what? We should be arresting Gabriel then? That *was* him in there." I stop, shaking my head and waving my hands in the air. "You know what? I can't even believe I'm talking with you about this. This is crazy. I knew this would be a dead-end."

"Like Trenton McAllister had?"

I whirl, pointing at him. "Don't even bring him up, Gabriel. Or Elias. Or whatever your name is! Just *stop*. I'll just let the police sort it out; I should have never come here." I start to walk away from him when he drops the second bomb that stops me in my tracks.

"Don't be a fool, Tracie. No one will believe you. *Not even Lela*."

My feet jerk to a halt, and my heart pangs with a cold fear. I slowly turn back around to face him.

Not even Lela. My beloved daughter.

"Accept the truth. This is all Moloch's doing. You're involved now. Moloch knows everything," he says. "I really encourage you not to interfere."

I swallow hard again while my heart pounds with the thrust of a steam engine.

He doesn't smile, doesn't blink, just watches me, solemnly. And I watch him. *Him.*

Gabriel. Elias. Moloch.

All of him, whoever he is.

"You leave my little girl alone. You don't even mention her name; do you hear me?" I demand, but my voice is tremulous, and it's obvious to him. He squints at me, and I can tell he hears my nerves. I back away, slowly, pulsing with fear at the sheer audacity of his statement.

Gabriel/Elias dwindles into the distance as I retreat backward to my car, finally pivoting away and screaming out of there. I never should have come.

I know that now.

9: THE FEAR

Present: **Sunday, January 10th 2021**

I'll never forget what he said to me.

I lay here in the dark of night, quietly stroking my daughter's hair as she snores gently next to me.

She's not too old.

Not too old to crawl into bed with her mama and be my snuggle buddy. I'll cherish these times for as long as I live, my sweet girl. The fact that Gabriel even knew her name just still unravels me to the bone.

I gently pat her on the shoulder, and she stirs in the night, whimpering slightly.

The winter moon graces her form, spilling down softly through the window slats, bathing her in train tracks of dim white light.

I yawn involuntarily as it's early, and I can hear the heat kick back on as we lay here, together. Lela has only had a few days of school so far, but she's a sixth grader now, and that's middle school. When I grew up, middle school was called "Junior High" at my school, Snoqualmie Middle, far over on the other side of the state. But they've changed it. In some places it's seventh, eighth and ninth. But at her school, Sacajawea Middle, it's sixth through eighth, and it's already been a bit overwhelming for her.

All the more reason for her to crawl in bed with her mama before she returns to school again tomorrow morning after an exhausting weekend. The spaghetti went down proper, as it always does, and the movie was fine – but I wasn't. I confess I was elsewhere, thinking about Gabriel. Thinking about Elias. Thinking about Moloch.

Remembering *McAllister*.

That tongue. Those eyes. That gruesome scene.

I needed to focus on my daughter this weekend. I owe her better than that. We need to schedule to have our nails done again, she and I.

What did Gabriel/Elias mean?

No one will believe you. Not even Lela.

How did he know my daughter's name? I always thought Elias to be the more innocuous and gentlemanly of the two twins, and Gabriel was the creepier one. But if that was Elias inside Gabriel, then they're *both* creepy as hell.

I truly think *Gabriel* killed McAllister and the others, no matter what 'Elias' told me.

Elias. I find myself missing him, actually. He was beautiful. He was strong. He was *innocent* of what his brother started. Moloch took that poor man, all because of some insane ritual and 'caring' gesture on Gabriel's part.

I can't suppress a sigh of deprivation, lying here. I'm already innately aware of my daughter's need for sleep, but she reminds me unconsciously with a sudden twitch.

I place my hand more firmly on her shoulder and give her a gentle shush, but in so doing I suddenly remember the spasm that Gabriel had. That 'Tourette's twitch.' And as much as I'd like to forget our exchange, with Lela's twitch I'm reminded of my conversation with Elias – at least the one of them that *said* he was Elias. There was no twitch there. None!

Maybe it truly *was* Elias.

I shake my head, subtly so as not to disturb my daughter. Could all this voodoo mumbo-jumbo be real? All this BS about Julia becoming Aadhya, and their dad, and that Hindu crap and incantations? I mean, could it *really... truly...* be… *true?*

Another sigh from me. Another stir from Lela.

How *dare* he bring her into this. How dare he even utter her name, literally less than one minute after he mentioned McAllister's name.

That bastard better not touch my daughter.

I'll kill him. I'll kill him so that he's dead once more, and can never switch bodies ever again.

The fury is boiling within me here in the dark, turning the room red with rage.

Lela stirs once more, sensing some disruption in the room. I'm scared to leave her alone; I'm scared to talk with her about any of this; I'm scared to see what may still happen within those walls. I feel like I'm the only one who really knows what happened, and I wish I could do something about it. But at what cost to me… and Lela?

I'm afraid. Afraid from the creepiness of it, afraid for my daughter, afraid for those prisoners in there, no matter what got them there in the first place. Afraid.

I took on a huge emotional load with all of this, and it cost me. I feel like I haven't been there enough for Lela. I *must* be there for my daughter.

No problemo. You have to do the hard thing, I'm here for you. You know that.

The words of the old Concepción hearken back to me, hauntingly, there in the dark. That wonderful woman, wise beyond her years. I have to do the hard thing, but so does Lela. She's heading back to school and dealing with all the trappings of puberty and teenager girls. They can be cruel sometimes!

I'll be here for her. I *will* be here for her, despite all this crazy voodoo hoopla. *I promise,* I whisper to her there in the dark, and Lela sighs in her sleep. I'm craving a smoke right now with everything that's in me, but I don't dare get up. I have to focus, and I just want to be here with my baby girl.

I have to remember what Concepción said to me.

10: THE GROWING

The Past: ***Wednesday, August 5th 2020***

They find another one.

I don't even get to talk to Elias. I'm here now reporting for duty, and everything is abuzz with activity.

"Another one bites the dust," they say.

"What? Who?" is all I can muster, glancing around in wonder and confusion.

It doesn't take long for the name to come up amongst the murmured reports through muffled, Covid-masked faces.

Elias Brickert.

He was in solitary confinement once more, but that didn't stop him.

They found him outside in the courtyard, staring up at a body. It makes no sense. I'm trying to gather information from the hubbub around me: various guards talking over one another in a mad attempt to get organized.

Now they want blood. And then I learn why.

It's Canton's wife. That's who Elias was staring up at. She was swinging, nude, hung from the supporting rafters of the watchtower on one corner of the prison courtyard. No!

Cathcart fills me in. Tamara Canton had come to drop off the superintendent's wallet; he had left it at home, they say. She brought it in and then went to the cafeteria to get some snacks. No one could find her for a few hours at least.

Then they checked the security cameras. There she was, naked as a jaybird, strolling around the prison, inmates whistling at her and ogling her. No one was with her…

…except one inmate.

An inmate that should have been in solitary confinement all along; in the hole, cut off from everyone else with high security around him.

Elias Brickert. Or Gabriel, or whomever the hell he is now. There he was, Cathcart says, in the footage with her, strolling down a corridor out to the courtyard. He, clothed in his prison garb, and she, completely undressed.

I watch Cathcart in horror as he lays out how they processed out to the courtyard, Elias seemingly 'guiding' her out to her final destination. She appeared possessed, Cathcart says, throwing herself against the walls of the corridor, scraping herself along the cinderblock.

At one point Elias handed her something. "What was it?" I ask Cathcart. *A knife*, he says. She takes it and carves a bunch of symbols into herself, clear as day on one of the cameras. But no reaction from her: no squeals of pain, no protests. Elias' face is clear as day too. She's lost her mind, under his spell.

He hands her a rope. Where he got it or the knife from no one knows. She takes the rope, swings it up to the supporting beams under the corner watchtower, ties it firmly, hoists herself up, secures it around her neck, pulls up the slack…

…and plummets to her death.

There she hangs, still. No one can get to her because she's out of reach. A fire truck is on its way with a ladder to get up to her, and they'll drive it into the courtyard and cut her down.

I can hardly believe it. I race outside to the courtyard between buildings, acutely aware of eyes peering out through narrow window slits of inmates fortunate enough to still take in imagery of green grass outside their cells. But they weren't fortunate to see this. No one was.

There she is. Tamara Canton, Superintendent Canton's wife. Naked. Hung. Blood-red. Dead. Interestingly enough, she still has a Covid mask on. I find that utterly odd.

Superintendent Canton isn't anywhere to be found. Cathcart's behind me and he says that Caleb's off with the prison counselor, Dr. Eggers. After seeing her hanging there like that, and after every conversation I've had with Elias and Gabriel… and after Trenton McAllister, I'm feeling like I should pay her a little visit as well.

A scuffle breaks out at the far end of the courtyard, and my eyes are drawn to a crowd of guards yelling. One of them, Travis, is screening off an inmate in orange. It's got to be Elias. Others are trying to get at him. Of course: there's Jones, Canton's nephew, also a guard here. Elias killed his aunt, and he wants blood. And then there's Westerfield: he's always got a hair up his ass, and he wants to join in the fray. Their voices ring out loud and clear, echoing off the cinderblock enclosure of the courtyard.

Travis is screening off Elias from the angry guards, warning them to back away. The warden is nowhere to be found. Everyone else is directly under the dead body of Tamara Canton, swinging in the early morning air of the prison, her blood still dripping down on them from above like a grisly red shower. Some of the guards that I happened upon when I first walked in are joining over to overwhelm Travis and get a piece of Elias. I run their way.

Cathcart yells after me. "Tracie! Tracie, stop!"

Travis pulls out his baton and starts swinging, yelling viciously at his colleagues to keep away from the inmate. "He'll pay for this, but not from you guys! Get back and let justice run its course! You don't want to do this!" he yells, urging them to let cooler heads prevail, but it falls on deaf ears.

They're a mob mentality now, and their numbers are being swelled by reinforcements of guards who passed me.

I can dimly make out Elias Brickert behind him, staring calmly up at the dead body. But it's not Elias in there. It's *someone else.*

Travis keeps swinging. The mob of angry guards keeps pushing toward him.

A shot rings out, and we all jump. I stop in my tracks, glancing around with widened eyes ringed with fear. Who even has a gun in here?

Only one.

Superintendent Caleb Canton appears suddenly as the crowd clears and shrinks away from him in fear. His right hand is suspended high in the air, his chamber still smoking from the round he fired. He glowers at the crowd as they pull away, beholding him in wonder and dread.

His eyes are red and puffy. Behind him stands Dr. Penelope Eggers, who rushed into the courtyard after him. She glances up at the dead body of her client's wife, and grimaces, shaking her head. I watch as she slowly voices something inaudible to the warden, gently grasping his arm to encourage him back into her office. She says it a few times, but the wind carries it away. He refuses.

Canton lowers his arm, still brandishing the gun. He turns over to Travis and eyes him sternly. Travis swallows nervously.

Caleb's voice is choked up and gravelly, but he's discharging his duty now instead of his weapon. "Bring him to processing. Do not lay a hand on him, *is that clear?*" The change in his tone as he redirects to his question is astounding and jarring. He loses it and yells the final part, and the guards who want a piece of Elias nod rapidly. They were just trying to defend his honor: that much is clear, and Jones, in particular, grits his teeth in frustration. He shares his uncle's dismay, but complies.

Caleb Canton retreats back in the same direction he came. Dr. Eggers follows him.

A honk sounds from outside the walls. The courtyard security doors swing wide, and in pulls a fire truck with the ladder to extract the swinging body of Tamara Canton.

The guards disperse, shaking their heads, backing away from Jones, leaving him to stand there, face to face with Travis. Jones' eyes are narrow slits of contempt, following every step that Elias now takes under the protective escort of Travis as he grabs him by the arm and leads him down the dark corridor.

But not before one final exchange. Not between Jones and Travis. Not between Travis and the other guards gathered there. Not between Dr. Eggers and Superintendent Canton.

No.

The cold eyes of Elias Brickert turn toward me, and I see Gabriel behind those eyes yet again. And for a chilling flash, I see Moloch in *those* eyes. I don't know how I see it, but I do. It's a displacement of the coloration… the temperature of the iris color, some primeval flicker, I don't know what it is exactly… but it's there.

He locks eyes with me and doesn't pull away until he is physically jerked away by Travis, tearing down the hall after Canton and Eggers.

The fire truck pulls in.

The wind howls on this warm summer morning, racing through the courtyard.

Tamara Canton is cut down. There's a lump in my throat as I watch them take her. Her body is covered in incredibly thin runes, carvings, symbols all over her. They look strangely Hindu in nature, which only serves to reinforce the belief that Gabriel/Elias was telling me the truth after all.

So many questions.

Where did Elias/Gabriel get the rope?

Where did he get the knife?

If Moloch is traveling around killing people in here, how did he jump from Elias/Gabriel and possess Tamara Canton?

How could she pull herself all the way up there and knot the rope herself?

Where are her clothes?

And how the *hell* did Elias get out of the hole again?

Or Gabriel?

Or Moloch?

This is all too much.

If Gabriel was right, then Moloch's power is growing, and he's able to hop bodies and do his thing in here. No one is safe.

I need to speak to Dr. Eggers as soon as possible.

Before they find yet another one.

11: THE CONFESSIONS

The Past: ***Wednesday, August 5th 2020***

I just can't believe it.

I stand here, watching him in complete disbelief. That can't be Elias. No. It's *Gabriel* inside Elias. And perhaps its *Moloch* inside *Gabriel* inside Elias.

This stuff is really starting to mess with my head.

Canton, Jones, and others who desperately wanted a piece of him have been escorted off and are being debriefed by the police. The other guards are back at their stations.

The rest of them are outside cleaning up Tamara Canton's body and carting it off to the coroner. The police are here taking stock of the crime scene. Various catcalls emerge from the different buildings – we can hear the collective lot of them through the cinderblock – ogling on the female police who are onsite. Their voices intermingle with those of the local news who arrived minutes ago, wanting answers and doing their thing just off the prison grounds, their cameras trained at their reporters and Airway. Word travels fast. Some of them are knocking down the doors of the main lobby, which has been secured and sealed. The institution is on lockdown for the time being. It's deplorable. No respect for the dead.

The whole environment has taken on a macabre sense of dread. We've had two deaths here in two days: both of them paranormal, both of them tied to one *Brickert, Elias James.*

There he sits, a cabal of security surrounding him in an interrogation room here at Airway, just outside processing. The door is guarded by other police called in once the situation proved to be a bit too chaotic for the prison to handle internally. The tempers are flaring, and we all know who wants a piece of this inmate.

Certainly not Dr. Penelope Eggers and Pastor Rosie Campion, also present in this tiny room, observing from the back and taking notes. They quietly exchange whispered thoughts between themselves.

Poor Caleb. He's going to be placed on leave for sure, allowed to grieve in his own way but relieved of duty pending an investigation into his wife's death.

And poor Tamara. That is no way for a person to die, especially her. I only met her once, but she was sweet as pie. She was near in age to her husband, and now my thoughts go back to dear Concepción: our wonderfully sweet babysitter. They were similar in age to one another.

Elias killed her. I can't believe it.

Is he really possessed? Standing here, watching him being interrogated by the Spokane PD – there are three detectives in there with him along with the two women, and the two police are stationed outside – I just find myself more than a little incredulous.

I'm trying to get a glance at his right arm. Elias has always had the scars cut into him; Gabriel the tattoos. Unless the tattoos covered *up* the scars. I don't know. Either way, my mind is inventing scenarios where Gabriel's tattoo – that creepy one of the two joined people – gets transferred to Elias' arm, and then I'd know for sure. But it's not there. It's just scars still.

"I didn't kill McAllister," is the first thing I hear him say. "I'm telling you the truth."

"Right," answers a blasé detective who has introduced himself as McDonald. He's the only one masked among them, but you can see his eyes sneering at Elias over the tip of his mask. The others have a cavalier attitude about Covid, apparently. Elias is masked. "You, the only one in the cell with him, didn't kill him. And I suppose you, the only one with the superintendent's wife early this morning, didn't kill her either. Do I have that right?"

"You have that right," he says to McDonald with a note of fatigued indifference. He's staring out the window now, detached from this conversation.

"None of this will fly in court, Mr. Brickert," barks McDonald. "You're gonna fry for this – you killed the *warden's* wife! They'll send you to the chair. You better start talking!"

"What would you like to talk about?" he asks coldly.

"Like – like how you got out of the hole – twice – and how and *why* you murdered those two people."

"I don't know. That's all I can tell you, and that's all I've been telling you. But you're not listening to me."

McDonald just stares at him icily. None of this is flying with him, and how much less will it fly in court. He turns and looks wearily at his contemporary, and then stands and paces around the room with his hands on his hips. Dr. Eggers gives him a halfhearted look of exasperation over her own mask.

"Your days in here are numbered, Mr. Brickert," says another detective, O'Hara. "You realize that, right?"

"No. Please enlighten me," Elias replies dryly.

"That was the supe's wife, man. You don't think this is gonna create extra restrictions around here, shrink things down a bit? Your uh, your cellies and neighbors ain't gonna take kindly to any further restrictions on what little freedoms they have left. They'll eat you."

"I hope I'm delicious," he says tiredly.

"So then, talk to us! How'd you get out of the hole?" O'Hara presses. McDonald turns back around and sighs, his arms crossed.

Elias stares down at the floor and shakes his head with a sigh for a moment. But his eyes don't stay there. He chuckles grimly to himself, and then raises two dark orbs at O'Hara.

"Magic," he breathes, and all I can see is Gabriel all over him. He smiles evilly, and it sends a chill down my spine.

Elias starts to laugh as they just stare at him in frustration and doubt.

"Welcome, Ms. Vossler. I'm Dr. Penelope Eggers – but you can call me Penny – and this is my associate, Pastor Rosie Campion." They both greet me with warm smiles. "Hope you don't mind us foregoing the whole mask thing for now. It's stuffy in here. Besides, we're too old; Covid wouldn't want us anyway." She chuckles.

I snicker in response. "I'm not sure that's how it works, but ok. I hate wearing them too. It's no problem."

Following the interrogation of Elias Brickert, I quickly connected with the two of them and asked if they had any openings anytime soon. Dr. Eggers replied emphatically that they could see me as long as it had everything to do with Elias – they were now required to prepare their own report based on their observations of him.

I'm in a melting pot of cultures now, sitting before the two of them. The prison shrink is certifiably British, with a thick northern brogue, while the pastor has a pronounced Mexican accent dripping with sincerity. I feel like I know them both from somewhere, but can't place it: they have a hint of familiarity to them somehow. Rosie, at least, certainly reminds me of Concepción with her Latin heritage.

"Thanks for seeing me on such short notice. Call me Tracie, please. How's Superintendent Canton, can I ask?"

Their demeanors both change, and they exchange concerned glances. Dr. Eggers speaks up first. "Well, to put it mildly, his life has taken a dramatic turn. He's resting now, relieved, but we should receive an update within the day, I should think."

"Yes," Pastor Rosie concurs, "he was quite shaken up. Everyone who saw it was. I think we'll be meeting with many. I was too, *Dios mio*," -here she shakes her head and widens her eyes, glancing over at Penny- "that was a horrible sight. Some things you just can't unsee, unfortunately. I'm sorry that the warden had to see it. But Mr. Canton will be back when he's well enough to be."

"Yeah," I say, fidgeting with my fingers. "You think you see every evil under the sun that lands people in here, but you don't expect to see it *in* here as well."

They both nod sadly.

"Well," Penny starts again. "You wanted to see us, you said? Something about the murder?"

"Murders," I correct her, emphasizing the plurality. "Yeah," I say, heaving a huge breath, "I have concerns that there might be something larger going on here. Something that everyone might have a bit of a struggle latching onto."

"Oh?" Penny asks. "What is that, precisely?"

I turn my eyes to Rosie. "Well, this might be more your purview, since you're the spiritual one," I say.

Both of them suddenly erupt into laughter as they look at each other.

"See? I'm the spiritual one!" Rosie says. "Note that down please, sister." She playfully slaps Penny on the shoulder, and I sense there's something I've missed.

Penny throws her hands up in submission. "As you wish, *Pastor.*"

I tilt my head in confusion.

"Oh, we were just discussing this this very morning," Rosie giggles, "about how working here requires an element of faith and trust in a Higher Power. You spend enough time in the darkness of the trenches, it can be hard to claw your way out, certainly. Dr. Eggers is not a woman of faith *per se*" -here she shields her mouth and leans into me, as if imparting a secret- "but don't tell her that her days are numbered and God's gonna git her!"

Penny hears her whispered secret, clicks her tongue, shakes her head and rolls her eyes. "Bollocks."

I like the two of them together. They make an interesting team, though ethnically diverse. "Faith and no faith. Acceptance and atheism, in the same room. Powerful combination."

"Indeed," Penny says, leaning toward me with wide eyes. She's the more delicate of the two: prim and proper, wearing a white blouse and gray slacks, gazing over overmagnified bespectacled eyes that make her poignant irises jump out at me. Rosie is sporting glasses as well, but she's wearing a purple turtleneck cable-knit sweater and polyester black pants, which I deem too hot to wear on this summer morning. "I let *her* do all the praying, and I get to stick to the sound guidance and proven logic," she finishes, and then turns to Rosie with a very British *hmmmppht.*

Watching the two of them, I swear they could take their act on the road as the Giggle Sisters or some other oddly named routine. They play off each other in perfect harmony, at odds with one another and yet in complete accord.

Rosie just shakes her head gently and smiles. "Well, now that we've over-introduced ourselves, my dear, why don't you tell us what's bothering you about this. We can help you through it as best as we can."

"Thanks," I reply. "I appreciate it. I'm not convinced that this won't sound crazy."

"I'll believe you," Rosie replies. "*She's* the crazy doubter," she replies, nodding toward Penny. Penny purses her lips and closes her eyes in mock-disdain.

"Great. Thanks. Well, it involves a bit of the – *paranormal.* I'm starting to think I'm a bit crazy too, here, watching it all unfold. And I wouldn't be so sold on it if I hadn't seen and heard everything I have so far. There's more to this than meets the eye, that's for sure."

"Tell us. Go on," Dr. Penny gently prods.

Slowly I lay it out for them: the strange tattoo, what Gabriel said, the Tourette's twitch, the conversations with each of them, what I heard in the visitation room, and the mention of Lela. I share everything with them as best as I can remember about the Brickerts' deceased Hindu mother Aadhya, and of the strange phenomenon that Gabriel described in such detail for me. *Bodhayana's Bhagava- something,* whatever it was.

Rosie slowly nods along, watching me with her fist under her chin propped up by one knee, while Penny takes notes at intervals on a legal pad over her crossed legs. When I'm finished, I just observe them, studying their reactions.

"I'm crazy, right? Or they are? Or… we all are, right?"

"Well, we're all a little crazy, love," Penny says, but this sounds quite on the margins, wouldn't you say, Rosie?"

"Oh *si*," Rosie says thoughtfully, elongating the vowel in *si*. "I don't dispute that there is something paranormal happening here and that the Brickert twins certainly could be playing with fire as it were, but that notion of this evil spirit – I won't name him – jumping between bodies is downright eerie."

"Right?" I agree. "I was most unnerved when Gabriel – or Elias, or whomever it was – mentioned my little girl." I stare back at them, and then hold my hands out helplessly. "Docs, he's never once met her. Not once."

"Fascinating," Dr. Penny says, observing me over the rim of her glasses. Curiously, Rosie is doing the same thing. "What do *you* believe, based on all you've seen and heard thus far?" Penny asks me.

I take a deep breath and exhale noisily, shrugging. "I mean, mentioning my daughter is one thing, but that was Elias right there on the cameras. I know it was him. He's gotten out of the hole twice now. I can't explain that. I also can't explain what I saw on Gabriel's arm with that tattoo. It would all seem like a bunch of weird coincidences if Gabriel – Elias, in prison – hadn't said what he said to me that night. *Greetings, Ms. Vossler*. Ick! It was so chilling, and it was definitely *Gabriel* inside Elias. If that's right, then one murderer is outside these walls while another has been brought in. It's all over my head how that could even happen."

"It is a conundrum, truly," Penny says.

Rosie is nodding her head, slowly, while staring at the floor beside me, lost in thought. "I wonder," she begins, "what this demon wants, if demon it is. There is always a motivation behind transference between this plain and the next."

"What do you mean?" I ask.

"Well, suppose this demon is here purely for mischief and murder. So be it. That is its motivation. But could there be something else? Perhaps some part of a greater plan? Rarely have I ever encountered spiritual realms colliding when there wasn't something grand at stake. Perhaps the twins are part of a bigger picture that Moloch wishes you to bear witness to."

"Why?" I continue, furrowing my brows. I can't imagine such a scenario being true in the slightest. "And why me? I'm nobody."

Penny clears her throat. "Hardly," she says, dismissing me gently. "You yourself have worked here, you've borne witness to evil. You've seen what these inmates can do, unbridled and in the throes of rage. It's human nature to go unhinged when one does not get one's way. Perhaps the Brickerts are just the beginning. Perhaps Gabriel, opening the door for this, this unsavory *Moloch* character, intended for more than to 'tie them together further in life,' as you mentioned he said.

"Yes," Rosie agrees. "I shouldn't make much of it, not much more than parlor tricks and lies, if not for him mentioning your daughter's name. If they had never met her and never researched you or known about you, only a spirit could know your daughter's name and invoke her."

A chill runs through my back. "Great. So, you believe them. The 'twinmates' at Airway. What a story."

They both nod, vigorously. "Clinically," Penny begins, "the psychology of it checks out. While I've never personally experienced transference of that caliber, or soul-jumping as it were, it's quite conceivable that whatever incantations their mother was pronouncing, it just might have worked."

Rosie nods in agreement, her hands clasped, perched on one arm of her chair. "Yes, I think it's best, Tracie, that you avoid them. *Both* of them. The very fact that you involved yourself may have placed you in this *demon's* crosshairs. Your daughter as well. All through conversation with the Brickert twins."

I sink a little in my chair, glancing around and biting my lip. Rosie notices it. "This is hard for you, isn't it. You have some sort of stake in this, I see." She's watching me closely over the tips of her glasses.

"No! No," I protest. "I just… I don't know what to do about. I mean… I think-"

"Hmm. I'm going to venture a guess," she interrupts me. Before I'm even finished nodding, she springs it. "You have feelings for them. One of them, at least. Correct?" Rosie looks at me sidelong with her eyebrows up and her lips pursed.

I steal a quick look over at Penny, and I feel like a deer in the jacklights. Penny also has her eyebrows up, and I swear one side of her lips is desperate to curve upward and reveal itself in a smile.

Is it hot in here? The A/C must have blown a fuse….

Penny can't hold her composure anymore. "Ah me! My dear, my dear. I know that look all too well. Geoffrey tried to feign disinterest with me, but I stuck a pin in his heart-shaped balloon and he was mine forever. Oh, he tried to remain indifferent! But the look of love on his face was plain as a pikestaff."

"Love? No way. I don't know what you're-"

"Oh, come now, *hermana,*" Rosie pleads. "It's obvious that you have feelings for at least one of them. I'm going to guess that it's the one incarcerated here, since you've seen him undoubtedly first, and *more.* I've seen him too. He's quite handsome. They both are!" She blinks demurely.

My cheeks feel hot, and I fidget. "Man. Was I that obvious?"

"No, you were just obviously *human,*" Rosie says. "Dear, we're surrounded by men in an all-male prison. We're women. There are fine specimens here, eh, Doctor Penny?" They giggle together momentarily. "It's alright to notice. But to fall in love with one of them-"

"I'm not in love! I'm *not* in love with him. Them. *Him,*" I correct myself again. I realize I'm digging myself a hole. "Am I?"

"It's alright, Tracie, your secret shall remain safe with us," Penny assures me. "And only *you* can answer that question. Rosie here has *plenty* of secrets on the men I've fawned over in here, oh dear me," she says, playfully fanning herself with her legal pad and lifting her eyes to the ceiling in a swoon. She suddenly corrects herself and extends a finger of warning. "But remember – to *look* is one thing. To *yearn for* – well, that's a slippery slope, Tracie, that you mustn't engage. It will end you, I promise."

"She's right, dear one," Rosie agrees. "They are handsome, yes, but given everything you've seen and heard, I would back off now while you are ahead, yes?"

I say nothing. It's still hot in here. I just purse my lips and nod silently, feeling like I'm back in Catholic school being remonstrated by the Bishop. *Oh, the trouble I used to get myself into…. That's partly why I joined the Marines…*

"Well," Rosie concludes. "I think we've said enough. Is there anything else?"

I shake my head, still biting my lip.

"*Esta bien,*" she says. "Dr. Penny?"

Dr. Penelope Eggers gazes at her colleague for a moment. "No, I think Rosie is right. Just this once, though," she says quickly, comically holding out her hand to stay us. She stifles a laugh. "Do be careful, Tracie. You're a guard here, entrusted to preserve order, not document it. To ensure it, not explain it. We shall take your concerns to the warden as soon as he returns, and the Deputy Warden in the meanwhile. We shall also include this in the police case file. They are awaiting our summary."

Do be careful, Tracie. Back off now while you are ahead, yes? I take those words to heart.

They study me, briefly. "Well," Rosie says finally, "thank you for letting us know. This is scary stuff, yes, but we're with you. And we're always here should you need to come back for any follow-ups. Here is our card. The numbers are our mobile numbers."

I take the card gratefully. Both of them are listed, one on each side, with shiny professional portraits of them on their respective sides.

"And Tracie," Rosie says, drawing nearer to me, "I know this is unnerving. Please know that I will be praying for you." She grasps me gently by the shoulders and squeezes me in comfort.

I take a deep breath and nod. "Thank you, Rosie. Penny, thank you as well. I appreciate it." They nod gratefully and study me as I walk out.

Prayer.

I can believe in that, at least.

12: THE UPROAR

The Past: ***Saturday August 8th 2020***

Things are somewhat back to normal now.

Elias is back in the hole, but he's sedated *and* in a WRAP system: like a straitjacket but more a full-body restraint, and he can be horizontal for sleep. They're not taking any further chances with him. He's been asleep a lot of the time, and fed intravenously while they keep him under watch.

I've stayed out of Gabriel's hair, though I must confess I did drive by Flint Crossing to ensure that he was there. I have half a mind to talk to his supervisor and inquire if he's acting normally or if there's been any change in his behavior of late: a sure sign that it's Gabriel inside Elias' body.

The talk with Penny and Rosie went well, and I've been trying to keep their advice front-of-mind over the past few days as I've just put my head down and gone about my business.

Superintendent Canton still isn't back, and they're preparing for Tamara's funeral. They're having a Celebration of Life, and many of us have been invited, though we have to pick and choose who can go due to staffing issues. I've neither seen nor talked with Caleb since he's been gone. Figured I'd give him some space.

For now, all is well before I report back to work tonight. It's a Saturday, and that means that I'm doing the graveyard shift… which means that Concepción is coming over for movie night with Lela and I before I head back into Airway.

I make a silent vow to myself to not enter the courtyard, and to not look up to where Tamara was hanging.

"I'm scared," Lela whines.

"How come, sweetheart?" I ask her, genuinely curious at her change of heart.

"I dunno… it's just a huge step up from elementary school. More classes, new campus, more of a headache," she replies, counting her complaints on her own fingers. "I don't know if I'm gonna be able to handle it. And I'm old enough to determine that social media would help me!"

"Honey, I get it," I say, as I feverishly mix up the spaghetti noodles, meat and sauce together. We decided on having spaghetti for our Friday night movie nights. We both love it, and we love making a mess with it as well. Concepción isn't fond of it, but she'll be eating her own ethnic food before she comes over for our movie night and babysits Lela so I can get back to work. A splatter of sauce splashes out and lands on my arm as I'm scooping too hard in my agitation. "I was once in middle school too, you know. 'Course, it was called *Junior High* back then, but still…"

Lela rolls her eyes, preparing for the inevitable *it'll be okay* speech she always thinks I'm about to give her.

"Seriously!" I say, catching her eyeroll. "Often times it's just the *fear* of something that ends up being bigger than the actual thing, ya know?"

"Mom, this is totally different. Things have changed since you were a kid. You didn't even *have* Facebook then."

"Yeah, and neither do you, sissy," I say. "Not yet, at any rate."

"Don't interrupt!" she lectures me, prompting a stink eye from mother to daughter. "You know what I mean! Social media. Instagram, TikTok, Snapchat, all of that. You don't let me be on *any* of those. What if all the other girls are and I don't even have a presence? No one will even know who I am!" She crosses her arms and huffs.

"Lela, you're too young, okay? We've talked about this. Let's not do this tonight. Please? Besides, I hardly think all the girls there are on all of those, honey. No parent out there is *that* dumb. It's a crazy world. Besides, all of you are gonna be in masks at school for a while anyway, right? You all won't even recognize each other. My answer is still no."

"Mom…" she protests. But no matter how much she does, I'm not letting her on social media. Not yet. I've heard too many horror stories. "I don't have to have all of them, I'm just asking for Snapchat, and you can monitor me with whatever *parental* thing you want, okay? Please?? I just wanna *look* is all!"

I just shake my head, speechless. I honestly don't know what to say that I haven't already.

And then it comes to me.

"Honey, you have to remember – to *look* is one thing. To *yearn for* – well, that's a slippery slope, Lela, that you mustn't engage. It could end you, I promise."

She just stares at me through narrow slits and furrowed brow, her mouth so agape I think bats might fly out of there. "What are you even *saying*?!" she pouts, and then my prepubescent daughter just sighs and slumps her shoulders, trudging off down the hall once more. I guess Will Smith was right all along: parents just don't understand.

Thanks anyway, Dr. Penny. I'll try using your lines on someone my own size. Or on Lela when she's older.

Or… maybe not at all.

I scowl, unsure if this new movie night trend is off to a good start or not.

"Come here, sweetheart."

I take her into my arms as she basically melts into me. Concepción smiles at the two of us, mother and daughter, as the opening credits of *The Half of It* roll. Lela just needed to burn off her angst and irritation; she didn't want to miss the movie.

Or her mom, I'm hoping. I know this mama didn't want to miss her daughter, despite the fact that Lela missed spaghetti by holing herself up in her room and being angry. Oh well. At least it gave me and Concepción a chance for a good chat.

She curls up into a ball and snuggles up against me. I smell her hair and squeeze her tight. "You hungry?" I ask. She shakes her head, staring quietly at the screen.

I stare down at her, compressed into a fetal position and nestled into my side, her cheeks resting on her own hands against me. She'll be fine. This, too, shall pass. After all, she's watching a teenage girl's movie, she's got her mama and her sweet babysitter nearby, as well as spaghetti if she needs it.

Beyond these walls, over the hillside, lies Airway Heights, and she doesn't know anything about what's going on in there. Her own little world is expanding, and it's quite big enough for her. She doesn't need to know about the horrors that I've seen in there. The less she knows, the better.

For now, it's just us, and that's enough.

This car can't go fast enough.

I'm screaming west on Highway 2. I'm almost to Airway. I can see the emergency lights flashing already.

Cathcart is on the phone with me.

Jones is dead. Elias is nowhere to be found. Jones' body was found mangled in a grotesque, distorted way – ungodly, misshapen, and without any regard for human decency – he was wedged into a custodial closet outside the main bank of cells in the R Building. He went missing and was not responding to his radio. They found him, sure enough, but he's gone.

Jones was the one who wanted a piece of Elias, and he was very vocal about it, even when Travis and he exchanged words since the killing of Tamara Canton. I don't know what may have recently happened, or what exchanges he and Elias may have had over the past few days – or even *how*, as he was apparently sedated for much of that time – but this is *bad.*

It's now the third murder in under two weeks' time! Jones' body was contorted into a ball, but his legs were bent backwards behind him, splayed up and over his shoulders, as if someone wanted to use him like a bowling ball. His ankles were hammered through with railroad ties into each side of his neck, and his arms were pulled tight behind him and stitched into his legs. He, like Tamara Canton, had had strange symbols carved into his flesh. Cathcart warned me against seeing it when I came in. He said I wouldn't be able to handle it. I think he's right. What is happening at Airway Heights?!

Elias is happening. Or Gabriel. Or both, that's who. And an evil spirit has control of one or both of them.

Moloch. He doesn't play nice with the living, and is making statements with each killing. *Gruesome* statements. Whatever he likes to do to his victims, it's grisly each time.

Fear is already concentrated and heightened in a prison setting. Maybe Moloch thrives on that.

I wonder if Penny and Rosie know. I wonder if Rosie is praying for the prison population. For Jones' family. For *me.*

My mind is racing just as fast as my car as I finally pull off Sprague Avenue and into the prison parking lot.

It's pitch black outside but for the spinning red lights and the towers with their spotlights searching the grounds. Everyone has been recalled if they've been off duty, and all staff is onsite. I bet Canton has been briefed even though he's not here.

Before I'm even fully inside, the speakers blare: *Inmate down, inmate down. Report to T Building.*

Another one?! My eyes are ringed with fear, and I wish I had a gun. Where is Elias in all of this?

Cathcart practically bumps into me as I grab a riot shield and baton and get ready to head once more over to T Building and see how I can help. He's frantic.

"Tracie, you don't wanna go in there!" he screeches. "Find somewhere else you can serve. Get with Delacourt and be on a search team. This one's grisly too, you *don't* wanna see it!" He's off before I can get any further information out of him. I have no idea where Delacourt is.

The prisoners' cells are cubes of protests all around us: they're already well aware of the frenzy of motion and the reason for it, and they don't feel safe. They have nowhere to go but here, and that's of their own making, but you can't help but feel sorry for them. Through the doors of the cells we're scurrying by, it's a flood of khaki-dressed inmates over gray t-shirts, staring out at us in worry and frustration. Some shout obscenities and plea for release: a plea we cannot grant or even acknowledge at this point.

Moloch seems to want to operate in the dark, in close quarters, and he's intentionally picking off inmates and guards in here. Very soon *intentionally* could easily morph to *indiscriminately.*

I swallow, a lump in my throat, not sure where to go. We're all combing the grounds for Elias when a *third* announcement goes up from over in minimum security, the C-4 unit. A call comes in to summon people to the admin building for the C-4 and C-5 units.

Inmates down, inmates down, guards report to C-3!

Inmates *plural*? I'm huffing and puffing, unsure which direction to go. Moloch is darting around here, ping-ponging between units and killing off prisoners for his own pleasure, and we don't have the manpower to track down some supernatural spirit.

And where the *hell* is Elias Brickert?

I'm whirling all around, staring in every direction in the courtyard between the main Medium Custody units. My head is reeling, breathing hard, unsure where to go. And then *another* announcement… this time in the N building.

And then in the K building.

My eyes are wide, and some guards curse as they run past, desperate to attend to prisoners but unsure what to really do about it.

Where are you, Elias? I ask. *Where are you?*

In a flash, my mind goes back to the initial killing, recollecting what I saw of McAllister's suspended body. On a hunch, I bite my lip, hoping I can trust my own gut, and I feverishly race toward the R Building, in near the complete opposite direction of where everyone else is heading.

Why? I don't know, but I hope I'm right. Or wrong.

R-41. That was Brickert and McAllister's cell before Elias got moved to the hole. It looms up down the catwalk behind the parapet, and the door is screened and cordoned off with yellow tape.

The power is out, and emergency power has kicked on. Whether that was Moloch's doing, or a safeguard was tripped somewhere, the building – outside and in – is drenched in black, and flickering with emergency lights strobing at foolish intervals. Not enough to see anything, and just enough to make you fear the dark in between.

The hairs on my neck stand up straight as I near the cell. As before, my knuckles grip my baton, readying it.

I'm at the door. I inch closer, slowly drawing my face to the cell door window.

I peer in.

There, sitting on the bunk with his eyes closed, facing me, palms up as if meditating, and yet covered in blood not his own, sits a man.

Elias James Brickert.

"Elias, what have you done?" I ask him, and my flesh crawls with tremors and bumps. I'm unnerved to a high degree, and just looking at him, sitting there, dripping, eyes closed, is surreal and disquieting.

His beautiful locks and muscular figure are crowned in crimson, and the dim light of the emergency lights flashing off of the walls glistens palely through the blood on his shoulders.

He opens his eyes, slowly, the haunting whites piercing as dim slits covered over by a sludge of red. Elias says nothing. Ripples of fear are tracing my back and my neck, and every hair on my arms is standing up. I'm gripping my baton so hard I may just snap it in half

"Hello, Officer Vossler," he says, quietly. There's no sinister smile on him like there was to Gabriel when they pulled him out of here after Trenton McAllister's murder. Nothing to suggest that this is in fact Gabriel. No *Greetings, Ms. Vossler.*

No. From his demeanor, his quiet, calm, eerie composure and simply the way he just greeted me, it's Elias. This is not Gabriel, I'm certain of it. This is Elias.

"Elias, tell me. Whose blood is that? Whose!" I already know, but I want to hear him say it. I want to *make* him say it.

"I think you know," he says quietly. "But it wasn't me, Officer."

"The hell it wasn't, Elias!" I screech, as quietly as possible, but it's no use. I'm fully aware there are inmates right next door to us, listening intently. "Don't give me that *Moloch* crap, Elias. It's their blood on *your* hands. Not Moloch's. No one will believe you! How are we supposed to defend ourselves against this in here? Tell me!" I'm banging against the door of the cell, no longer caring about the noise. My conversation with Penny and Rosie is ping-ponging around in my head right now but sounding as loud as a gong. *You have feelings for him, or for one of them. You love him.* I do have feelings for him, but right now they're swallowed up in pity and pleading.

Suddenly, below and behind me there's a great ruckus. I whirl around as the main doors to the R Building burst open, with Delacourt at the head of a guard procession in riot gear. He's flanked by several of them. I can see Cathcart in the mob. They're shouting and splitting up. I spin back around to Elias.

"Elias, why? *Why* are you doing this?"

"I'm *not* doing this, Tracie," he says, and there's panic and sadness in his expression. "I am innocent," he declares, and his lip quakes while his eyes plead with me. "I swear to you."

"Elias…" I breathe, and I feel more love and sympathy oozing out of me, but there's nothing I can do. He's a handsome man, and he's been simply caught up in something that his brother started. He might even be innocent of the crimes that sent him here! Maybe Gabriel committed those crimes!

Come on, Elias, you've got to break free of this. "Elias, they'll never believe you. You'll go to the chair for this! I swear it."

"So be it," he says without a beat. "Then I hope to take him with me. That's the best that I can do."

"Who? *Who,* Elias? Gabriel? Or...?" I know who he's talking about, but I don't want to say it.

Cathcart calls my name. I've been spotted. They're getting closer. They've split off to each side and are coming up each gangway to the upper level, closing in on cell R-41. When they find him in here...

"Elias, you've got to have Gabriel come in, you've got to have him explain it.... They'll never believe you, Elias!" I rail at him. "Please!"

"It wasn't supposed to be this way... I... I don't know what else to do but to give in-"

"No!" I shout. "You can't give in, Elias. If it wasn't you then you can be declared incompetent to stand trial, or... or something!"

And it's then that he smiles. But it's not out of joy or gladness. It's not out of peace or closure. It's out of pity and resignation to his fate. Whether it was Moloch or Elias himself who murdered them – or Gabriel in Elias' body – he's got to talk to them, maybe even Rosie and Penny together, as I did, and explain to them. Surely there are tests that can be done!

But right now, Elias James Brickert doesn't care about that. All he wants is to be done with it. "Gabriel was only trying to help me," he whispers, the blood dripping from his lips, running down his hair into his eyes, as he blinks stupidly and closes them once more, squeezing them tight to shut out the blobs of crimson that come oozing out of his eyelids.

"Elias," I whimper helplessly...

"I'm sorry, Tracie. You've been good to me. To Gabriel. And thus, you've been good to *Moloch!*"

In a flash, just as the guards arrive and thrust me aside, desperate to get in there, corner him and haul him away, Elias James Brickert roars out. It's not a human roar. Otherworldly, it's filled with bass and a terrifying vibration, and yet there's a high-pitched dissonant shriek blending into the hurricane coming from his soul. My skin crawls and tremors run down my spine. His brow furrows. His mouth is agape. His teeth are drenched in red. The whites of his eyes are exposed as widened circles as he opens them again in panic and alarm – and malice – but only for a moment.

The door is hurled open. The guards never make it inside his cell.

Elias' body completely dissolves into the pool he's been sitting in, and fragments of his flesh trail off in sparking hot embers drifting on an embattled wind. They flash and flicker and then go out like dying fireflies, tracing off in random directions, while the rest of him melts into a vile ooze that comes rushing out at all of us in a flood. Some of it splashes into my mouth; I taste iron and smell metal. In a retching reflex, I spit it out and cough, backing away against the railing.

So do Cathcart and another guard. It's Travis. They flank me, grasping for purchase while the tide of decrepit evil rolls over us, bathing us in warm filth. It's more blood than can fill a man; maximized and multiplied, flooding out from the cell as if from a limitless reservoir. It surges over all of us, throwing Cathcart and Travis over the railing as they plummet to their death below. The cracking report of vertebrae sounds out loud and clear as they meet their maker on the ground floor of the R Building, covered in a waterfall and deluge of blood which coats their lifeless bodies.

My head is spinning as I sit there with eyes ringed with fear, face coated in blood not my own. Around me, all the guards are retching and gagging, spitting out whoever's blood they just choked on, dry heaving from it all.

Elias James Brickert has disappeared entirely, and with him, the truth. Gabriel is out there somewhere, and he *might* be able to explain it. But whether he can or not, he's guilty too. He had some part to play in this. He started all of this, and it was *his* incantations that ushered in Moloch.

If nothing else, I have to speak for Elias. I have to get this information to someone else who will listen. But who? Not the FBI or the police. They won't listen. Not Superintendent Canton; he's got his own troubles right now and he's still grieving.

Not Penny or Rosie; they'll just call it psychobabble and offer bumper-sticker-worthy assurances while professing that they'll pray for me. Maybe not Penny, but Rosie would.

No. Someone else. I've got to go digging and find someone who can trace this all back to the source and deal with it there. Otherwise, Elias – wherever he is now – will never be free of what his brother did to him.

His brother. There's only one who can explain it, and only one who might be able to reverse it.

Gabriel Titus Brickert.

He's really, truly, the *only* one, and I have to find him.

Things will never be the same again.

PART THREE: THE DEFIANCE

13: THE OUTSIDE

The Past: ***Sunday August 9th 2020***

They won't let us go.

There's an APB out on Gabriel. The police haven't found him yet. They need to, and I need to. He's the only one who can make sense of all of this. If only I could find their *mother* in all of this too. She would certainly know the incantations and could possibly restore balance. But she's dead. Perhaps she left that journal somewhere with her incantations in it. Perhaps Gabriel still has it maybe?

Everyone – *all* of us – are on lockdown in here with the prisoners. Every one of the inmates in R Building who stared out of thin windows, rooted to their doors in horror as Elias exploded and surged toward them: locked down as well. The bottom floor of the R Building is covered in blood, and that slow crawl of crimson wormed its way into many of the nearest cells. The inmates were screaming. They were terrified, climbing up onto the highest bunk and calling out for help.

We can't leave. We're not allowed to. The Feds are here and the news has caught wind of all of this. I can't even get home to Lela. Thank God Concepción is with her and had a free schedule! It *kills* me to not be able to see her.

It's so stuffy in here *and* we still have to wear our Covid masks. Irritating. Can't breathe. I'd kill for a little outside time just to be able to breathe freely, but we're all in a rotation and it's not my time yet.

It's been fourteen hours since Elias' incident. I've been able to talk with Lela over the phone at least: that's *something*. It's more than the guys in here get. Their loved ones hear rumors and crazy stories of 'something happening at Airway' over the news, but they can't verify that with any of the inmates in here because there's a blackout on phone usage during a lockdown of course. Fights have broken out in the cells between inmates incensed that they can't leave. Even over in work camp, in the MSU Buildings, they're confined to their tiers with multiple guards stationed there.

Staff has been reinforced and the police presence has been huge. It's the first time in Airway's history that we've had a regular presence of police officers intermingling with the prison guard staff and posting up in stations. I don't know when it will end.

Thankfully, the guard staff has also been reinforced, and we've taken on transfers from other institutions in order to supplement our own men, considering the fact that we've lost some of them. I'd call all those guys crazy who decided to come work over here. *Man.* You'd have to have a death wish to work at Airway right now, in my humble opinion. Word travels fast, and there have been killings here: *several.* They've stopped, at least for now – presumably because Elias has disappeared, and with him Moloch, but the lingering specter of fear hangs heavy over this place. Maybe Moloch has had his fill for the moment. Maybe he truly wanted to only get back at Jones, and others got in his way.

I've never been in such a scene of pandemonium. Thank God Airway has showers for all the guards, because those of us in the R Building desperately needed it. The poor guys who were already on cleaning detail had the mops and sponges working overtime cleaning up that filth. It wasn't just blood. It was floppy tissue and slippery entrails in there: clotted sinews and clumps of God knows what else. And it wasn't just in the R Building, of course.

Jones was a mess… an absolute revolting mess. I didn't see it, as Cathcart advised me not to. I didn't *want* to. Poor Cathcart. He had to go out seeing Jones like that, and then he had to die after seeing that whole scene with Elias. He was a good man, he really was, and I'll miss him.

It's quiet now, finally. Where Elias went, we don't know, if he's even still alive. Who knows.

Penny and Rosie have been working overtime counseling many of the inmates who were traumatized by that. One particular inmate, Valenté, doesn't speak any English, and kept calling out in Catholic prayers *Dios Mio, Dios Mio!* Thankfully Rosie was there to speak calm into his quaking Latin heart.

The call comes in at just before noon. I grab my cellphone and answer the unlisted number.

The voice is weak and quiet, but I know it's him. It's Gabriel Brickert. He doesn't tell me where he is, but he voices instructions to me, calmly and methodically.

You want to see me. And I want to see you. I have answers. You've received clearance to leave.

I'm fazed by that – I hadn't submitted any requests for special clearance; we're all on lockdown and *no one* has received any clearance to go anywhere. The place is crawling with Feds anyway.

But how will I get out? How did you-

There's no time now. If you want answers, I need to see you. Just head out like you normally would.

OK.... where am I going to meet you? And you realize this call is being recorded right? We're on full lockd-

No, it isn't. You must trust me in this. Meet me at the coordinates that have been sent to your phone.

I look down at my phone. An unlisted number has sent me a text. *47.684799, -117.638529.* Those are GPS coordinates, sure enough.

Go. Now. Or you won't be able to. *Click.*

A creeping thrill runs down my spine and tingles all over. There's an unshakeable feeling that I'm being monitored. I don't know quite where I'm going, and I don't know what will happen to me when I get there. I have half a mind to just go home to Lela and get the hell out of Dodge.

But the compulsion for answers is too strong…

Apple Maps has it out in the middle of nowhere. *Great. Of course.* It pulls up somewhere off North Rambo Road northwest of Airway.

I'm scratching my head how I wasn't even asked any questions upon my departure. I just flashed my badge, scanned out and walked right past the front desk and a bunch of cops and Feds intermingling. It's like I was a ghost. They didn't even acknowledge my presence. I literally walked right past them…

…until I bumped into Rosie out in the parking lot, that is. *Hello, Tracie,* she greeted me cheerily. She expressed no surprise that I was outside Airway in a lockdown, showed no confusion at my demeanor or quick dismissal, and invoked no Airway Heights policy reminders. She literally just grinned, walking right past me into the prison.

Moloch is doing things, I tell myself. *Moloch is not just limited to a single person, if everything Gabriel told me is true. He's moving in and out of people, influencing them if he wishes, having them do his bidding and commit his murders, and paving the way for something...*

The landscape scrolls by my car, silently. I'm almost to the rendezvous point. I cavalierly note to myself that it's hard to steer and chew your nails at the same time.

I decide to call Lela on the way. She hears the subtle din of road noise in the background and eagerly asks if I'm coming home. I have to disappoint her with a resounding *no, I wish I could, sweetheart.* I can hear her palpable frustration and aching sigh make their way through my earpiece. "I promise I'll be home as soon as I can, sweetheart. I swear to you. We're still on lockdown."

"Then why are you driving somewhere?" she prods.

I bite my lip. I obviously can't tell her the truth of the matter. Aside from the fact that she'll call me crazy, it could get her or me in trouble. "It's hard to explain, honey. I'm – I'm being taken to a place to speak with a witness." That's the best I can give her, and it's at least partially true – I *do* feel like I'm literally being *taken* to meet Gabriel.

"Someone's taking you somewhere? But you're in your car?"

"No, I'm, it's-" -my throat catches and I clear it- "honey, it's better if you don't know, okay? At least for now."

"Mommmm," she moans. "What's going on, tell me!"

"Honey, dammit, I can't, okay? Please just trust me for now, okay?"

"One dollar," she whispers, quietly, dejectedly.

All I can do is grunt. *The profanity fine again.* She caught me. "Okay, fine, I owe you a dollar, sweetheart. I promise you I'll be home soon to pay up. As soon as I can. Okay? *Promise.*" This is heart-wrenching. I don't even know if I can keep any of these promises.

There's a lull in the conversation as she ponders the weight and integrity of my sworn word. "Fine," is all I get, in an equally dejected moan.

"Can you put Concepción on for me please?"

No answer. Soon, the babysitter's on the phone. "Miss Tracie, are you okay?" she asks in earnest.

"I'm fine, Conchita, thank you-"

"I've heard about everything on the news. I promise I'm not letting *mija* see it." From the recesses of our apartment, *I heard that* sounds out. Concepción chuckles. "Are you sure you're okay? Is there anything I can bring you while you're in there?"

I sigh. "I dunno, maybe a six-pack of Coors Light and a hot masseuse?"

"Oh, *Dios mio,* I don't think I could, Tracie…"

I give her a nervous snicker in response. "I'm just teasing. I'll be fine. There's just something I have to do."

"Something…" She pauses, uncertain. "Are you driving? I thought the prison was on lockdown, no? I'm confused, are- are you coming back here?"

"No, Conchita, not yet. I just have to see somebody. It's about the… whole…" I trail off, unsure how much to clue her in on.

"Miss Tracie?" Concepción ventures, but her voice drops off. I don't know what to say and just keep my mouth shut, allowing the heavy lull between us to form a blockade. "Well, *esta bien*," she whispers. "I've got *mija.* Don't you worry about a thing, ok? We'll find something nice to watch and we'll work on our beautiful beads, that's all. You be careful, yes?"

"Yes. I will. I promise. Give my baby girl a squeeze for me, will you? Hopefully they'll let us go home tomorrow."

"I hope that too. *Te amo*, Miss Tracie. *Hasta la próxima.*"

"Hasta la próxima," I reply, and she clicks off.

Sigh.

I'm here. There's nothing around me except for flatland and sparse trees: evergreens, mostly, although there are a few poplars. The ground is scorched manila in the heat of summer. Fading green still clings to the dry trees around here, mostly at the stumps where the occasional rainwater collects.

Other than that, it's an abysmal, dryad calm, and no one around for miles.

Exactly the kind of place where I would be meeting some nefarious wanderer and his murderous spiritual tag-along.

The trees seem to whisper to each other out here; there's no other sound except for that and the pounding of my heart. At any minute I expect to feel fingers wrapping around my neck and throttling me from behind. Thankfully, Rosie's prayers must be working, because it's just me.

Until it isn't.

A few short paces from the coordinates – Apple Maps almost took me right to it within twenty feet – there he is, stepping out from behind a cracked tree stump. He must have been watching me approach.

It's Gabriel. Or Elias. Or both. I can't tell anymore. He's not covered in blood as Elias was in that cell. But he's still creepy as all get-out.

"Hello, Officer Vossler," he says, calmly. There's no sinister smile, no deceptive mug, nothing to conjure up fear in me or denote any kind of murderous intent. If we'd bumped into each other out on the streets of Spokane, I might take him simply for a kind stranger.

But I know it's him. I just can't tell *which* one of him. All I can do is take a modicum of comfort in the fact that there was no *Greetings, Ms. Vossler.* And with that, I'm convinced – however unlikely it must be – that I'm staring at Elias. I don't know how, but it's Elias. Which can only mean that Gabriel has body-swapped him and is back there in the prison… *somewhere.*

"Who are you?" I plead, desperate for the truth.

"We've had many names over the millennia," he says coolly, stepping out from behind the tree and pacing slowly my way in a wide semicircle, still giving me a decent berth. "We take whatever name suits us."

"Us?" I ask nervously.

"Us," he restates.

"That was you in there, operating through Elias. Wasn't it?" A smug half-grin. "You killed all those inmates and guards, Moloch. You're a murderer."

He appears to scowl slightly. "I hardly think that now is the time or place to hurl accusations, so far removed from civilization with no one to hear you."

That was a threat. I squint at him, trying to maintain a stoic visage, but the chilling statement disassembles me.

"What do you *want*?" I ask him. "And… why me?"

He studies me, coldly, foot to crown, sizing me up presumably for some cold, devilish purpose. Moloch squints at me and opens his mouth as if to speak, but holds his tongue for a moment as if pondering. "Suffice it to say that there is something about you, Ms. Vossler. Is there not? You are attracted to the Brickert boys, are you not? Truly, your heart has been pulled toward Elias at least, and you feel for him. You have compassion for him."

"I suppose so, sure," I attempt to dismiss him. "But what does that-"

In an instant, he is right in front of me. I yelp in alarm as a flicker of his persona where he stood blends into a static flash and burst, and there is a haunting trail of vapor behind him as he materializes right in front of me, eyes cold with a demonic heat.

"Don't deny it," he says coldly, his orbs piercing into my soul. I feel paralyzed, though he's not touching me and there is no physical contact between us: a good six inches of discomfort linger between us. I don't think it's his intent to kill me. My heart tells me that he wants something else, here, standing unnerved before him. The air takes on a sudden, biting chill around us.

I'm no longer confident which Brickert brother this is, but maybe it isn't either. Maybe it's entirely Moloch. Maybe it's been Moloch all along.

"You love him, do you not?" he pushes, and I see no point in denying it.

I don't know what to say, and fear to say too much. "Love is a bit of a stretch. I'm… *attracted* to him, yes," I say between fearful pants, trying to appear calm before his piercing gaze cutting my confidence into ribbons.

He sees right through me and clicks his tongue, wagging his head from side to side. "You are not being truthful with me, Ms. Vossler. Do you not understand that I am of the spirit realm? I see more than you can possibly fathom, my dear."

My dear. At those words my flesh crawls and my panting turns to shivering. It was hot, and now it's as cold as a meat locker around us. It's then that the sullen truth hits me squarely in the face and I almost pee my pants in cold fear: I am speaking directly with neither Gabriel *nor* Elias, but with a demon.

"Moloch," I say, -here he grins slightly at my acknowledging this true name- "what do you want me to do?"

"Thank you. Now we can speak plainly." The chill lessens, and I know then that he was causing it. "There remains a bit of unfinished business that I must settle before I depart this plain. A certain matter between myself and the woman called… *Aadhya.*"

Aadhya. The Brickerts' mother. The one they once called *Julia.* "Elias and Gabriel's mother," I whisper.

He doesn't respond.

"It is with Aadhya that I must reckon," he says, lowering his face and staring at me grimly under his brows. "There can be no peace until that is done."

"But," I start, my head shaking both from disbelief and from the lessening but ever-present cold, "she's- she's dead. How can you reckon-"

"I have certain… *abilities,*" he assures me with a devious grin, and a chill runs down my spine once more. "You have borne witness to them at your prison, have you not? I have enjoyed my recreation there."

Recreation. The murder of human lives.

"And," I swallow, trying to force the words out, not daring to move, stand still, run… anything, "what happens if you can't… *reckon…* with Aadhya?"

Moloch's expression becomes downcast. He turns from me slowly and walks back to the tree that he emerged from. He stops short, not turning back to face me. A cold breeze kicks up and dislodges some fallen leaves and scattered patches of grass. "Then there will be a certain… *unpleasantness.*"

I swallow hard. He means more murders, certainly, and then he clarifies it for me.

"Indeed, it's been very unpleasant there of late, no?" He revolves slowly back around, and whether he had it in his hands this whole time or not, I don't know, but it looks like a forensic file folder. "I learn from only the best." He slowly approaches me, arm outstretched, the file folder offered to me. "Take it."

I'm nervous as all hell, but I do as he asks. Who am I to oppose a demon, anyway? He hands the file folder to me.

"Open it."

I do so, slowly, fingers trembling. The police report has the incident dated June 19th, 1993. There's a picture of someone clipped to the police report who looks at first glance eerily like the Brickerts. Of course: it's their father. There's the name: Brickert, Kieran Icarus. *Odd name,* I think to myself, but now I know where the Brickerts get their oddness, perhaps even more so than from their mother.

I flip the page and without warning I see it. My stomach lurches and I instantly choke back vomit.

A sickening scene.

A body: contorted into a ball, its legs bent backwards and up, splayed over their shoulders, as if someone wanted to use him like a bowling ball. Strange symbols are carved into his flesh. His ankles have been hammered through with railroad ties-

Railroad ties! A bowling ball! Cathcart told me that Officer Jones was killed in exactly the same way! I raise my eyes to Moloch in alarm. "You've done this before?"

But he shakes his head.

"I presume you can read, Ms. Vossler. The assailant is named right there in the file."

"Your father, Kieran," I breathe.

Moloch shakes his head again. "No. *Their* father. I simply learned from him."

"So… what are you saying?" I ask him, still reeling in my stomach. "That your- their *father* was the real villain all this time, and not their mother? Not Aadhya?"

"That is for you to figure out."

"But both are dead."

He shakes his head once more. I'm growing a bit tired of that. Moloch puts his back to me and stares off toward the horizon.

"You know," he utters, changing the subject, "your Airway Heights facility is a wonderful hunting ground. Especially during this virus climate. This 'Covid' terror has certainly set the stage in ways I could never have anticipated, granting me an ideal hunting climate. Fear is maximized already. More so in such close quarters. And it is all the greater when the overwhelming majority of the occupants cannot escape. My prey cannot even flee," he breathes, a sadistic pleasure spreading his lips wide. "I will enjoy my continued recreation there."

I have to stop him. But how? How can you compete against an evil, transient spirit that can come and go at will? How can you defend against such a being? I have no idea what he even wants me to do. "Moloch," I plead, but the words don't come. Nothing comes, except for a desperate desire to get the hell out of there-

The being turns back around suddenly, and there's Elias' eyes once more, his childlike visage staring out at me from behind the demon. His eyes beseech me. "Aadhya lives." My mouth drops open. "In the Seattle-area. She is hidden from me. But you will find her and kill her before she can conduct the ritual that will banish Moloch." It's Elias speaking now, but he's in a daze, almost puppet-like: Moloch is using his voice and mouth to speak. "Your Elias must be returned to the prison I'm afraid."

Aadhya lives?! Gabriel told me that she was dead. Where could she be? And I can't kill anyone! "Hey," I plead once more, shaking my head and holding my hands up, "I- I'm no killer. I can't kill anyone. Please."

His forlorn expression is further downcast, and his eyes fall to the ground, shaking his head in sadness. He heaves a great sigh. "Then," he starts, about to pronounce some great doom, presumably about further murders at Airway, "I'm very sorry about Lela."

Elias' expression instantly changes back into a sinister sneer as his eyes flick back up at mine, which are now ringed with fear and anger. Moloch is jumping in and out of him, but now the bastard is back. My teeth grit. A protective swell courses through me and my fists clench. "Don't you dare touch my-" I start to hiss at him.

Before I can register the weight of it all or fire off any potent backlash, Elias' body collapses, folding over itself, leaving only the quiet husk of one of the Brickert twins lying on the forest floor. I was moving toward him, but I stop short and yelp. I'm unsure of what I should do. The cold is instantly gone and I'm once more standing alone.

The body is motionless before me. Is he dead? Is it… Elias, reformed? Or Gabriel, back to himself, devoid of Moloch's presence?

I'm very sorry about Lela. My daughter. I must protect her… but how?

The body moans, returning once more to consciousness.

Elias? The spirit has left him, and he's returned? Can it even be? I rush to his side to find him lying there on his back, stoic, eyelids fluttering in the light, his hands spasming erratically. I cradle his head in my hands, and the warm feeling of supporting his skull feels nice. *Stop it, Tracie… you're yearning…* He blinks stupidly, looks around, gathering his bearings before finally raising his eyes to me.

"Where-"

"Shh, don't say anything. You're okay now. It was Moloch, Elias. *Moloch.*" His eyes open wide in alarm, and I can hear him gasp, though it's guttural, as if some residue from Moloch still resides in his throat or something. He suddenly props himself up on his elbows and looks around fitfully. "Your brother did some kind of incantation from your mother's journals, and- and- I don't know, *something*. Are you okay? Are you… *you*?"

He looks around, blinks, and nods. "Yes. I'm me. At least… I think I'm me. And I know of the ritual."

"Can you stand?"

He slowly nods, and I help him to his feet. I look around sheepishly, worried that someone will spot us. I am out of my mind to be out here with an escaped convict. *I'm gonna be on the news… right before they send me to the slammer, that is.*

But I smile at him and realize again that he truly is handsome… especially without all that blood drenching him and flowing over his shoulders. Gabriel is identical to him, sure, but there's an edge to Gabriel that is lacking in Elias. "Good. Well, I have good and bad news. You're back, and that's great, but you're outside the prison, Elias. You've gotta go back."

He doesn't utter a word. He just stands there, surveying me, resigned to his fate, and – I daresay, *humbly* – accepting it.

"I'm sorry," I say.

"Me too," he agrees with a quiet nod. The wind kicks up for a moment and sends his locks flying around him. He squints into the wind.

"It's just protocol, nothing personal. It's-" I pause, not wanting to tell him this, though I'm sure he already knows it. "It's not going to be fun, Elias. It isn't. None of it. Those guys in there want your head, especially since you, I mean, *he* killed those people. They want blood, Elias."

He nods, again, quietly, his eyes fixed on the ground. "I understand. Let's get it over with, please, Tracie."

I stare at him and can't suppress a sigh. It's like this thirty-three year old standing before me is only ten years old, caused some fresh hell and now has to go 'fess up to his mom about what he's done. It's almost unbearable. How could Moloch prey on someone as childlike as him? How could he use this man to do his bidding when he's so handsome- I mean, so innocent? *Dammit, Tracie, get ahold of yourself!*

I take him by the arm, and he doesn't resist. I help him into the back seat of my Altima, knowing full well there's no divider there, and if Moloch inhabited him once again, he could easily overpower me with a simple chokehold, sending my car spinning off the road into oblivion with me in it.

Elias Brickert is in my car. And if that's true, where is Gabriel? If he is at the prison somewhere, have they found him? And if nowhere, then where is Moloch now?

One thing's for certain: I must find Aadhya. I *must.* I don't want to, and I've certainly no intention of killing her as Moloch instructed, but I've got to find out what was done, and see if there's a way she can undo it.

For Elias and Gabriel's sake.

For Airway's sake.

For *all* our sakes.

And – with a lump in my throat because of the threat that still resounds in my head and heart from that evil being – for *Lela's* sake.

He *must* let her go.

14: THE PRESENT

Present: **Monday, January 11th 2021**

I see now.

The truth was staring me in the face all along: I loved Elias James Brickert. I barely knew him, but I felt for him, and perhaps that pity got morphed into love.

He was handsome, I'll give him that, but there was something alluring about him. That allure only grew exponentially after I learned more of his story and met his creepy brother. After I saw his eyes and witnessed that obscene event in his cell. After I spoke with him and drove him back to Airway.

I'll never forget it. They arrested him onsite, sedated him once more, and a guard even got in a few punches, beating on him until he bled. Elias took all of it, almost as if he felt it was his fate to bear the brunt of all the anger and displeasure of Airway. The look in his eyes…

Those eyes: they still speak to me. There was something crystal clear in them. Cerulean… alluring… tempting. I wouldn't call it *innocent* anymore; I've seen his file. But I felt so bad for him as they practically pulverized him when I came back in.

And oh *boy* did I get reamed out when I got back. I was suspended pending an investigation then as well. Seems like all I ever do anymore is get in trouble since the Brickerts waltzed into my life. The only good thing was that I got to have another few sessions with the Blister Sisters: Penny and Rosie. I gave them that moniker because *this* time, they blistered me. *Giggle Sisters* just didn't seem to fit anymore.

I told *you not to yearn,* Penny leveled at me.

Deputy Warden Dylan Whitmire reamed me out and sat me down under a glaring light with excruciating questions. All I could tell him was the truth, and that wasn't good enough. He didn't want to hear *Moloch this* and *Moloch that,* as he said. It was truly frustrating.

Lela's in school now, so I'm alone with my thoughts today: alone to reflect on how I circled the drain and spun out of control, lost my self-esteem – even lost myself. I put my job on the line and my very *freedom* in jeopardy by pursuing this even though I was counseled not to. I'm still wrapped up in it, though I long desperately to escape it.

And now here in 2021, Elias is dead, Gabriel is out there, Moloch is somewhere only God knows where, and I'm having my feet held to the fire over something I didn't even do.

Worse than all that, though? I still struggle. How could I not? The guilt eats at me, and those other men's blood is on my hands.

I have a long list of regrets now. I wish I would have trusted my gut. I wish I understood Moloch better. I wish I wouldn't have played with fire.

In the end, I foolishly did *exactly* what he wanted me to. Moloch *wanted* Elias back in that prison. And I, stupidly, gave him exactly what he wanted. With Elias out of the prison, he couldn't 'ride' him in there, and kill again. I inadvertently delivered to Airway the precise conduit that Moloch needed in order to continue his murderous rampage.

And kill he did. Over and over again.

I squint my eyes in frustration and sadness, and the tears come once more.

I will never forgive myself for it.

15: THE TROUBLE

The Past: ***Monday August 10th 2020***

Here we go.

I knew it would come to this. After the dust settles with the Deputy Warden, security, and another briefing by the FBI, I'm put back in the lockdown and under an active investigation.

It doesn't matter that I didn't go *out* with Elias Brickert; I came *in* with him, and I'm therefore guilty by association. Fraternizing with an inmate is a felony, and they could send me to Purdy women's prison for that. It doesn't matter at all what I say or what I'm simply relaying from either Elias or Gabriel. I'm already guilty in their eyes, and, thus, my job is on hold pending this investigation.

Gabriel still hasn't been found, but now they've got Elias sedated and under armed guard once more, monitored and wired up with electrodes. They even brought in a paranormal investigator, or that's what Penny and Rosie tell me. It seems like they're not taking any further chances this time, and perhaps one of them heard a tiny seedling of my story and decided to cover all their bases. If there's any kind of paranormal activity around him, they'll know. Maybe.

Thank God for Concepción. She was able to stay over again and see Lela off to school. It pains me to my core that I can't be there with my daughter. My mind is going back to her every five minutes, and my fingernails are posterchildren for anxiety; I am chewing them down to the bone. I'm nervous, I'm afraid, I'm anxious over her, and Concepción isn't ever quick enough when I text her to ask how Lela's doing. Lela herself can't answer me because she's in school, and they have to surrender their phones.

So, I had to call in a favor to Big Shirley. She works here, of course, and technically should be here on lockdown, but with her age, they made an exception and let her return home. She doesn't live too far from Lela and I, and I was able to call her and ask that she watch the school for a while. Thankfully, she was happy to. You can take the people out of the guard at

Airway, but you can't take the guard out of the people. She's ex-military too, so she was only too happy to help, though all I could give her were cryptic references to potential harm to my daughter. That was enough for her, and she's more or less on stakeout to ensure that Lela doesn't go anywhere she isn't supposed to.

So – that's a relief.

But now, once more I'm sitting stoically before the *Blister Sisters*: that's what I've decided to call them, given their penchant for telling me exactly how it is, and not holding back.

Because they don't.

"Oh, dear Tracie," Penny says, her head in her hands. "Dear, dear Tracie," she moans, and then stares at me with disapproval. "I warned you not to yearn, did I not?" I look over at Rosie mournfully, and she's got her lips pursed and staring at me over her thin dark frames. Beady eyes of conviction strain outward toward me. I don't feel judgment or disappointment from her, but she's obviously alarmed at the turn things have taken.

"I'm sorry! What can I say?" I offer. It doesn't help.

"Look, Officer Vossler," Dr. Penny says in a huff. "We're both up to our eyeballs counseling inmates traumatized from the incidents of only two days ago. They're *still* scrubbing blood out of the crevices of that building, don't you know? And then, here you come, bumbling back in here with the very suspect wanted for all those murders, and you can't even tell us how you – *or he* – got out of lockdown in the first place? Codswallop."

"What?" I say, unfamiliar with the term.

"It's British for *poppycock*. Forget it," she says sternly.

"Isn't *poppycock* also British?" I argue, not even sure why I'm doing so.

Penny purses her lips and stares daggers into me, saying nothing. I swallow hard and sigh.

"Look, Tracie," Rosie begins, "obviously things have taken a turn for the worse. Elias is in very serious trouble. This inmate is highly dangerous, and you're attracted to him. We already know that. When this thing goes to court, the two of us will be asked to testify over what we knew of your relationship with him, and we'll have to tell the truth, yes? You're making this very hard on all of us."

Suddenly, a swell of frustration courses through me. "Look, I don't have a *relationship* with him! I didn't ask for *any* of this! I'm caught up in it just like you are. Just like we all are! All of this is such BS, and I just want to get home to make sure my daughter's safe, okay?"

"But if you-" Rosie starts.

"No!!" I interrupt. "I told you – all of you – what I know. There's something going on here beyond what we can all see, and unfortunately this Moloch guy thinks I'm a part of it, or- or *wants* me to be. I don't know! I just want to be home with my daughter." I slap my hands down hard on the arms of the chair that I'm in, facing them in some kind of hostile inquisition. I hold my head in my hands in an exhausted resignation. I truly want out of here.

Penny glances over at Rosie and sighs. Rosie just shrugs. There's an awkward silence that settles over us, as if one of them is deciding how to pronounce some great doom for me.

But it doesn't happen that way.

"Tracie," Rosie finally says, "I have been praying for you. I want you to know that. It feels, from everything that you've said – if you are of course telling us the truth–"

"I am."

"Okay. It truly feels as though you are in great danger. If this Moloch person is to be as feared as you say, and if your daughter has been mentioned by him, then I would counsel you, once again, to drop this. I do not care what Mr. Brickert said to you concerning the twins' mother. It is not your affair anymore. I would counsel you to surrender the information to the FBI and just sit tight while they take care of it."

"And if Moloch doesn't let them take care of it?" I pose, though she has no answer. She starts to speak, opening her mouth, but ending in a shoulder shrug.

"It's not your affair anymore," she reiterates. "I don't think it ever was, really."

I look to Penny, who stirs.

"Rosie is right, Tracie. You're in over your head. You're a security guard. You're operating outside of those parameters. You are *no* detective, love. You have been entrusted with the security of Airway Heights from prisoners, not the entire physical plain from evil demons. You are in over your heart and operating outside of your paygrade. That much is readily apparent to both of us." She glances over at Rosie, who nods grimly.

"And if Lela has been threatened as you say she has, then you need to be with her. What we will recommend is for you to be released from employment for the time being and dismissed from lockdown so that you can be with your daughter, under strict orders that you not contact either of the Brickert brothers."

"I agree," Rosie says. "You're in this too deep, Tracie. You need to take a step back."

I inhale a massive amount of air into my lungs and hold it. Of course they're right, but not when you take into account what Moloch said. He personally asked *me* to find – and kill – Aadhya. Not that I have any intention of doing the latter, but I want to at least find her and talk with her. For everyone's sake.

"You're conflicted, yes?" Rosie asks me. "I can see it. Brickert told you something – or this *Moloch* did – that has you somewhat stuck in indecision. Tell us."

I let all the air out and shake my head, turning away from them and covering my mouth in thought. They will *not* accept this. There's no way. And they certainly wouldn't approve of or endorse it either.

Fine, I think to myself.

"Moloch wants me to kill the Brickert's mother," I breathe, just about as passively and nonchalantly as I can.

"What?!" Rosie screeches at the same time Penny's mouth drops. The doctor flips through the file she's holding over her knees, quickly searching for something. "Elias said that to you?"

"No, Elias didn't. *Moloch* did. Moloch wants me to kill her."

Rosie looks flabbergasted. "Using Elias' mouth. When you were out there with him beyond the prison walls," she asks. It isn't a question, but instead comes across as a passive-aggressive indictment.

Now I've had it. I roll my eyes. "Look, I was just doing what I was told. It's not like I was trysting with him, or- or, having sex with him, Rosie. He called me! And he asked me to meet with him. Please, both of you, credit me with a little more sense than that!

"Rosie!" I rail at her. "Don't you even remember I passed you on my way out? You *knew* we were on lockdown, Rosie, but you didn't even say anything to me when I was walking out! Don't you see? This Moloch guy means business! And somehow, he's able to control what we see and hear, who gets where, and, and, I don't know – just makes people do what he wants! He made it so that you didn't even register that I was leaving lockdown!"

Rosie just blinks at me as if she doesn't recall. Either that or she's starting to see the light just as I am.

"Julia Rosetta Brickert is deceased," Penny breathes, staring down into her file. "It's right here in Elias Brickert's paperwork."

I shake my head. "No. That's what the twins say. But that's not what Moloch says. Maybe they don't even know, themselves. He specifically said that she's alive, and that she needs to be killed before she can, I don't know, pronounce some incantation that will contain him. Or… something."

"And he asked you, *personally*, to do this?" Penny says, eyes wide, leaning toward me. She's incredulous.

I nod.

"And what will happen if you do not comply?"

A heavy sigh from me again. "I- I just don't know. But he specifically mentioned my daughter. He said he was 'very sorry about her.' If that isn't a threat, then I don't know what is!" I slap the arms of the chair helplessly again.

Rosie and Penny look at each other in deep concern.

They're starting to get it, finally, I think to myself.

An unbearable length of time passes. The room suddenly feels like it's making its presence known: stuffy and disquieting. A cloud ostensibly passes over the sun outside.

Finally, Dr. Penny flinches and then breaks the silence. "Oh, sweet, Tracie. We're sorry for you. We know this is hard for you. Elias Brickert is truly an attractive man. A little fascination with him is just fine. You mustn't punish yourself."

I just stare at her, frowning. That wasn't her voice. It's almost like she had a change of heart, or… or some other will is striving with her own. She continues.

"We'll make the recommendation that you be released on your own recognizance so that you can be with your daughter. Just do let us know if mister handsome inmate comes calling, okay?" She giggles.

Dr. Penny winks at me playfully. I squint at her. Seeking reassurance, I glance over at Rosie. Rosie is offering a wistful smile, as if all is well with the world.

My eyes dart back and forth between them.

"Hold there, love," Dr. Penny instructs. She retrieves her handset and dials. "Yes, Warden's office? Dr. Penelope Eggers. Yes, thank you. Is this Dylan? Oh, hello, Dylan." She covers the mouthpiece and then turns toward Rosie. "It's Dylan," she says affirmingly, as if the two of them are sharing a secret adolescent crush. "Yes, Dylan, I'd like to arrange for Officer Vossler to be released on her own recognizance so that she can be with her daughter. There's been some concern that she's been off by herself. No, she's with a babysitter but Pastor Campion and I feel that Tracie here would be best suited to be away from the present environment so that she can attend to her daughter. We have our hands full with the inmates and the ongoing crisis anyway. Mmm-hmmm. Wonderful. Alright, thank you, I'll send her your way. Thank you, Dylan!"

She gleefully hangs up the phone, and all of it seems so very theatrical and dainty. Dr. Eggers turns back to me, a glazed-over smile plastered across her face. "Well, that's that. You're free to go. All's well as ends better, eh?" She sticks her tongue in her cheek and winks at me again.

I'm unnerved. The warmth in the room gets sucked out as I realize the gravity of what's happening.

Moloch. Moloch is in here with us. My eyes search around in fear as a chill runs down my spine.

"Do touch base with Deputy Warden Whitmire on your way out so that you can fill out the proper paperwork."

"And good luck!" wishes Rosie, nodding at me and winking in turn. "You'll be fine. Keep us posted, *si*?"

I nod, reluctantly, but my chin practically slams into the thousands of little raised bumps on my arm, all protesting in unison at this eerie turn of events.

Moloch is here. He's doing this.

I fumble through my words, thanking them, rising, and getting the hell out of there.

I walk out of their office, not turning back. I won't turn back. I don't want to turn back.

Moloch is there, and I'm leaving.

It's time to go.

16: THE RAMPAGE

Present: **Monday, January 11th 2021**

It was horrible, all of it.

He killed twenty-seven more people that night. I had no sooner stepped over the threshold than the alarms went off. I banged on the front windows, but my pass wouldn't work, and

Judy at the front desk wouldn't let me back in. She was up, scampering away and running off toward danger.

And then I saw him holding her severed head. Then – the flash that saw me peeling out of there in my car, and screeching for home while Moloch conducted his violent rampage inside Airway Heights, using the innocent conduit of one Elias James Brickert.

They had him constrained, straitjacketed, confined, muzzled, and sedated. Nonetheless, he woke up. With horrifying strength, he disabled his captors and smashed through the room, appearing and disappearing at will throughout Airway, killing at will.

And I'm the one who brought him there.

I'll never forget going home that day, August 10th 2020; I've never held Lela more tightly. She whimpered in my grip. I thought she might pop, I was constricting her so much. I didn't know how much I needed to hold my baby girl. I needed her to know that she was okay; I needed *me* to know.

It's been five months since that murderous rampage. Five months of living in prolonged fear and not having answers. Five months of knowing that I brought Elias back in there, Moloch took hold of Penny and Rosie, and I was allowed to walk free out of there so that Moloch could have his way with Elias doing his bidding inside that prison, while I could be free to do his bidding *outside* it.

I can't sleep. My daughter is safe… for now. But none of those men were. The night I was released on my recognizance, I came home and held Lela tight. I had intentionally shut off my phone off because I didn't want to hear any of it… didn't want to hear from Airway… didn't want to be involved anymore… didn't want to risk Moloch calling me and making me meet him somewhere. Regrettably, however, I ended up sneaking a peek at Apple News on a bathroom break, unbeknownst to Lela; curiosity was gnawing at me.

It was all over the news.

Guards slain. Inmates brutally murdered. Grisly descriptions littered the article from what the news media had been able to gather, stationed outside the prison.

Glasgow smiles carved into inmates faces, slashed from the corners of their mouths to their ears.

Intestines removed and makeshift nooses formed with them. The victims' arms had been cut off at the wrist, preventing them from untangling the noose and freeing themselves.

Decapitations. I think once more back to Judy. *Poor Judy.* But it didn't stop there. There were victims' heads that had been replaced with *other* victims' heads, stapled together in crude, macabre haste.

One victim's skin was entirely removed and flapping in the heat of a fan in a break room. The body was chopped into pieces and organized into strange symbols across the floor like a demonic chessboard.

Another few inmates strangled with their Covid masks.

The fragile cigarette between my fingers trembles as I remember back with horror.

One guard, who had only just started employment at Airway the week prior, was found burning like a torch, melting after being doused with oil. Where the oil came from, no one knew.

Another few were stripped naked and intertwined with each other in the fashion of a ghastly game of Twister.

And finally, multiple inmates, stuck within their cells with nowhere to escape to: their bodies had been turned completely inside out, and the entire inner walls of their cell were coated with blood and plasma, as if they had been suddenly inverted.

I nearly vomited reading it. I could have been one of those victims. No names are listed, but inmates *and* guards were mentioned as victims. There was no word from Deputy Warden Whitmire. The news had reached out to Superintendent Caleb Canton, but there had also been no response from him.

At one point, texts from Concepción started loading once my phone was connected again. She was worried; many of the same reports were on the news, and she wanted to know if I needed her to come back over. She knew all about the rampage.

The whole world knows about the rampage now. It was all over the news.

And the most chilling report: my fingers traced the words, scrolling downward, downward, until I found it:

Police do have a suspect in custody, but are not releasing any names at this time.

They got him, at least. Elias.

He was murdering inside the prison once more, having been possessed and used cruelly by Moloch. Either that or it was Gabriel in there, having body-swapped with him, and Elias was outside again. I remember slamming my phone down and clutching my temples at the sheer insanity of it all, finally reaching for it again and shutting it off.

There, sitting on the toilet with my head in my hands while Lela occasionally asked from the living room if I was alright, the questions bounced around my head like a violent and wicked ping-pong game. They wouldn't stop, as I sat there and shivered in fear.

Is Moloch really truly real, and if so, can he be 'banished' as he said? Can he actually be stopped?

Is Aadhya really still alive somewhere?

If so, does Moloch know where?

How would I even go about killing someone? I can't!

Are the FBI on to me? Do *I* have a file now?

Did the Brickert's father, Kieran, really kill that man in the same way that Jones was killed?

If so, what does that even mean for the Brickert twins?

What made Rosie and Penny change so? It had to have been Moloch in there, twisting them for his own ends.

What will they do to Elias?

And where in all this is Gabriel?

But, most importantly, how can I even protect my daughter through all of this? How can I possibly shield Lela from a *demon*?

I was consumed by worry, and my nails were truly paying for it. I was crying softly into my own hands, trying to shield the sound from my daughter. I finally splashed some water on my face with trembling palms, trying desperately to compose myself as I attempted to return to Lela out on our couch. We were talking and catching up, and enjoying it. But I wasn't even mentally there.

I never should have turned on my phone. I tried desperately to listen to my daughter as she brought me up to speed on her 12-year-old middle school life, but I was lost in a thousand-yard stare for much of it, and she noticed.

When I *was* looking at her, she asked me at one point if I was okay; my focus felt like I was seeing right through her, scrolling that news feed again, my eyes glazed over and detached from the conversation.

I couldn't maintain it. I burst into tears. She asked me what was wrong and hugged me. I told her it would be okay and gave her the good ol' trusted, *mommy's just dealing with some stuff right now.*

Those poor people…

And my poor Lela! I should have been rejoicing that we were together, but I let myself get sucked right back into it. She had heard rumors of what was happening at Airway. I did my best to dismiss them and assure her that everything is fine. But it wasn't fine. None of it.

And I'm part of this, whether I like it or not.

I take a drag on this smoldering wick, and it's all I can do not to cough and retch, the carbon monoxide mixing with my horror and fear.

All I could do was beckon my daughter to me once more and sigh from my soul as she sunk into my embrace and just allowed me to hold her… hold her… hold her… both of us trying to purge away the fear.

The fear of what happened five months ago.

But not just that.

The fear from what followed.

I had to talk to him, no matter the consequences.

That's when it all would go south for me.

It would be horrible, every single part of it.

17: THE DISOBEDIENCE

The Past: ***Tuesday August 11th 2020***

I'm interfering, and Moloch is getting to me.

I can't help it! I *must* talk with Gabriel, regardless of what the crazy Blister Sisters tell me, and regardless of how much they scolded me before they went politely berserk.

So… that's precisely what I do. But not before I fetch my Sig Sauer P365 from high up in the kitchen cabinet, and then retrieve the bullets from the bottom drawer of my dresser.

The text comes in: I've got confirmation from Big Shirley that Lela is okay; Shirley is stationed once more outside Sacajawea Middle School, watching and observing. I can only pray that she's both vigilant *and* not called to report back into Airway, leaving me with no one to watch Lela in my absence.

My mind is racing; I feel like I'm back on some military op, being thrust back into action. I strap on a hidden belt and holster and handgun behind my back, like I'm some FBI agent about to put on a blue blazer. My windbreaker will shield it from view at least.

It's a Tuesday, and, normally, if he's anywhere, Gabriel would be at his job at Flint Crossing. But wait - he *shouldn't* be at his job, right? I mean, why would he be? There's an APB out on Gabriel, after all.

Unless he's back there in prison, and that's *Elias* out here somewhere. But no; I would have heard about it by now. There is no person with the last name *Brickert* to be found inside Airway. This body-swapping confusion is starting to really piss me off.

I think back. Where is the one place I've met either of them outside of prison?

Think, Tracie. Think. I try to breathe, calmly, centering myself.

I remember!

With a flash, I'm back in my car and tearing back up the road to those GPS coordinates out in the forest once more.

Quiet.

That's the one word I would use to describe this placid forest. The air moves lightly through the trees, and it's a hotter than average morning for Spokane in the thick of summer. Thankfully, those last coordinates are in my Apple Maps history, and I'm here once more.

But there's no trace of any of them. No Elias, no Gabriel, no Moloch. In the distance, I can hear the remote sounds of foresters and machinery humming from somewhere, out on errand conducting their business: logging or otherwise.

I'm roughly at the same spot I was before. He doesn't show. I've got time, and decide to do a little Googling.

Julia Rosetta Brickert, Seattle, Obituary, dated October 12th, 2003.

I'm surprised it's still indexed in the search engines, but I do a little more digging. There's not much to be found other than the same name and date reference, but search results are no longer generous with the archived details.

Except for one. I see her. It's Julia, aka Aadhya. It looks like a wedding photo. It's grainy, yet thankfully in color: a studio portrait of a man and a woman in marital bliss. They look young. The man in the photo is nearly a spitting image of Elias and Gabriel. And the woman's delicate facial features are there, though muted by heavy mascara. I strain my eyes, but I can definitely see a resemblance to Gabriel and-

"Hello, Tracie."

I yelp and turn to my right, dropping my phone in a reflex, covering my mouth. "Elias?" I brandish my handgun, aiming it straight at him. Elias steps out from behind a tree, just as he had done before.

He nods, holding his hands up in defense. "It's okay, I promise."

"Like hell it is. You scared the crap out of me." I bend down to retrieve my phone, clutching it against my chest, seized by fear, my gun arm remaining trained on him. "No BS now; which are you: Gabriel or Elias? I need to know the truth!" I plead with him.

"It's me, Tracie," he assures me. "It's Elias."

I just stare at him. I can't see his right bicep to confirm if that bizarre tattoo is there, but even if it was, I'm not sure that I would take that at face value anymore anyway.

"What the *hell* is going on, Elias? This is getting way out of control. And why aren't you Gabriel out here? Don't they have *Elias* in there?"

He nods. "They have my body, yes, but it's *me,* Tracie. In Gabriel's body. That's what Moloch does. I can't control it," he says, continuing to hold his palms up in defense. "Moloch does what he does and rides us as he wishes."

I just stare at him. "So, was that you or Gabriel that just killed all those people at Airway? I mean, I have very little sympathy for the prisoners, Elias, but those guards-"

"I know. I know," he says, shaking his head. "I'm sorry, Tracie. It was… my body, definitely. But you have to believe me when I say that I'm not in there when it happens. I'm in *Gabriel's* body."

My eyes inadvertently squint at him, staring over the barrel of my Sig Sauer. "Like right now, you mean."

"Yes. Gabriel is in my body in there, but my spirit is out here. Moloch is with Gabriel."

"So," I ask, frowning, "what does that even mean, Elias? Does that mean that whenever Moloch enters the picture he pushes you out and rides Gabriel?"

"Yes!" Elias hisses, appearing desperate to convince me. "That's how it's always been."

I'm not convinced. "But how come you, like, exploded that one time? If that was your body, then how are you even inside the jail, put back together again, Humpty?"

"I don't have any answers. I wasn't the one to do the incantation. You must remember this was all Gabriel's doing. He's the one who ushered in Moloch accidentally."

"Accidentally, huh?" I ask, accompanied by a pronounced scoff, "the more I see with all this garbage, the more this all looks to be on purpose. And why is your mother still alive anyway?"

I'm not prepared for what happens next.

Elias' face visibly brightens in surprise and alarm. "She's… alive?"

Suddenly, the weight of it all comes crashing down on me. Gabriel is not the squeaky-clean brother he presents himself as. He's creepy, sure, but he presented as a law-abiding citizen and was not the one incarcerated. It was him that invoked Moloch in those incantations, and probably on purpose. And even more upsetting than that, Elias' eyes tell a story of misery and heartbreak: Gabriel has told him, all this time, that his mother was dead.

He repeats himself. "Tracie… please. She's alive?"

The pity is coursing through me as I perceive what happened between the two of them. "That's what Gabriel told me," is all I can say. "But yes, Elias, Moloch told me that she's still alive. He told me that when he possessed you out here, last time I talked with you in this very forest."

Elias' eyes drop to the ground, lost in thought and memory over his apparently undead mother.

"Elias, you've got to give me something to go on here. Throw me a damn bone. How can I talk to Gabriel? How can you get him back out here and you be in your own body in there?"

His eyes raised up to meet mine in alarm. "I can't go back. After all those murders…"

"I didn't say it would be easy. But I'm not bringing you back through a procession of people who are going to beat on you, man. Your body is already in there. So, I have to find out how to get you back in it so I can talk to Gabriel. Moloch wants your mom dead."

"Dead?" His head tilts and his eyebrows furrow. "Why?" Elias' voice contorts to anguished disbelief.

"I don't know! He said something about killing her before your mother can pronounce some incantation to banish him."

Elias blinks in confusion.

"Is that not true?"

He shakes his head in a tremor, searching for explanations, for rationale, for *anything* to explain the madness of all of this, but he's speechless.

"Elias…"

"Wait," he says, "I know how you can send me back."

"Go on," I press, still with the gun trained on him, but my guard has relaxed now that he's willing to indulge me.

"It- it only happens when we're both sleeping. That's when Moloch can enter. At least, that's what Gabriel once told me."

"Gabriel told you that?" I press. "How would he even know that?"

He frowns. "Because he's seen it before. Remember? He's done this before, Tracie."

Suddenly, in a rush of recall, time whisks me back on a memory curve to that conversation I had with Elias after McAllister was murdered. He specifically breathed, in a lament, *Gabriel opened the door again. He's back.*

My mouth opens. Of course. "Gabriel let him in the first time," I whisper in truth. Elias nods slowly. "When, Elias? When!?"

"When our dad was killed. Back home. In our house in Seattle. He- he was practicing some of mother's spells. He wasn't supposed to, and he knew that. Dad caught him. Gabriel grew angry, and, I think he- he kil-"

Elias stops, but he doesn't need to finish the sentence. I already get it. *Gabriel killed his own father.* Or, rather, he allowed Moloch to enter him and kill Kieran Brickert.

"Elias," I whisper to him, "if that's the case, then somehow, *somehow*, your mother was able to banish Moloch after that. She was able to banish him! I mean, how old are you now? You're thirty-three, right? Your father died when you were eight. The day your mother took you to the carnival."

Elias slowly nods his head. He appears fatigued, and his eyelids slowly open and close as he does so.

"That's twenty-five years of hibernation, Elias. Somehow, your mother was able to banish him, to trap him back in… wherever. I don't know. Your own brother is sabotaging your own mother, Elias, and she is still alive. Moloch wants me to kill her."

Elias's eyes flick back up to meet mine in alarm and incredulity. "No. No!"

"Yes. That's what he told me. So, if he's riding Gabriel and pushing you out, then we have to get you back into your own body and find your mother. We can stop him, Elias. Together."

His eyes flutter momentarily. He actually suppresses a yawn. "I'm sorry," he breathes. "This is all a lot to bear."

"I know. I know," I say. "First things first. How do we get you back in there?"

"I have to go to sleep."

"Okay. So, what, do you need a place to lie down? I can get you in the back of my car again-"

He shakes his head vigorously. "No. No, you don't understand. I have to lie down as *me.* My own body – with Gabriel currently in it – has to lie down and sleep in Airway. That's part of the problem; they keep sedating me, and when that happens, Moloch is able to body-swap us and ride Gabriel into Airway. So, *Gabriel* – in my body – has to go to sleep in there to force Moloch out. But it's the not what… can't do I make with…"

His speech is slurred.

"Elias?" I ask him. He shakes his head briskly, widening his eyes. They're blurry and red. His face appears drawn. "Elias, what is it?"

"I don't… am… know, just so tired all sudden of…" Elias slowly lowers himself to the forest floor and feebly places his palms underneath himself to steady his body in comfort. "Just for a minute…"

"No, Elias – you can't!" I start, moving toward him. "You have to stay awake, Elias."

"Mother…," he moans, and that's the last thing that he says before passing out completely.

It's no use. I shake him, and he doesn't respond. "Elias? Come on, wake up." Nothing. "Elias!" I holster my weapon and kneel down on the ground beside him, peeling open one of his eyelids. They're dilated. "Damn!" Now I'm faced with the prospect of heaving his muscular body up into my car yet again. I look away from him, sighing, my head in one of my hands.

Movement. Only slightly, but it's there: a flicker of something to my right, on the ground. It's sudden, almost imperceptible, but I see it, as if two tiny points of amber fire have ignited below me.

A chill mist flows through the forest, and the bumps on my skin raise in response. I slowly move my eyes over to Elias.

His eyes are opened, and glowing with a creepy fire, a flickering amber hue.

But they're not his eyes. Not anymore. They're *Moloch's* eyes. I yelp and start to pull away, rearing up and reversing back toward my car. He starts to rise, glowering at me from under his eyebrows. I raise my weapon.

"Elias! Stop!" I cry. It's useless. He advances slowly toward me. "Don't come any closer, I'll shoot – I swear! Elias!"

He stops, staring at me icily. I'm panting, my heart racing inside my chest and pounding through my ribcage. A tremor shoots through me as I train my gun on him with a frenzy once more.

But all he does is smile, staring at me with that smug expression of his. It's Elias' face, but Moloch's malice.

"You should have done what I asked, Tracie. I warned you. Now your daughter will pay the price. Goodbye."

A pang of fear washes over me, giving immediate rise to anger and vengeance. What am I waiting for? He smiles again, cruelly, wickedly, and my finger flexes on the trigger. "No – no!" I cry, and can't restrain myself. My mama-bear instinct kicks in, and my index finger pulls the trigger back repeatedly.

Elias vanishes with a cackle, and my bullets meet nothing but air. They ricochet harmlessly off tree stumps and rocks littering the forest floor.

In a panic, I rip myself out of there, throw myself into the driver's seat and kick up dirt, screaming out of the forest and back onto North Rambo Road. I have *one* place to go, and one place only: Sacajawea Middle School.

Twenty-six frightening minutes away.

My hands are trembling as I fetch my phone and speed-dial Shirley. A chicken wanders out onto West Deno Road, and I look back up and swerve too late. The car thumps and skids, and a plume of feathers erupts and balloons in my rearview mirror. In a flash, I see Lela's face in pain.

My gut screams horror, and I gun the gas pedal all the way to the floor of the car. *No, no, no, no,* I whisper to no one in particular, my eyes streaming.

I reach the intersection of West Deno and West Trails Road, and there's a backup. Some slow-traveling camper van is blocking me. I skid off road and nearly lose control, flying out onto Trails and clipping a motorcycle. I'm screaming now, in hysterics. The motorcyclist gets up and runs off the road as his bike gets smashed by a speeding SUV.

You should have done what I asked, Tracie.

His voice reverberates in my head, sounding accusation after accusation, remonstrance after remonstrance, and I'm self-recriminating through hot tears.

"Shut up!" I scream. I don't want to hear Moloch. "Come *on*, Shirley, pick *up!*" I'm screeching at the top of my voice, redialing and redialing. Nothing.

Lela's face once more.

I break off Trails onto North Flint Road, and, mercifully, there are few cars dotting it. At least until I get down to Highway 2. The housing complex and the Hilton Garden Inn pose a bottleneck of cars at the confluence with the highway, and I have to gun it, pushing my car past its forte, racing around them, bouncing over the curb.

"Come *on,* Shirley, pick up *please!*" My mouth is dry and my throat catches. I'm about to go ballistic, and my mind is racing with dreadful scenarios. Call the school? I'd be stuck in voice mail jail. What's the damn main line number for Paula at the front desk? I scream to Siri to look it up. She doesn't understand me and offers information on a bowling alley.

"Dammit!"

That's not all I say. I would owe Lela a cool thousand bucks for the profanities I'm slurring right now. My poor Lela! *Please, God, let her be safe!* I pray. I briefly think back to Rosie, wiping tears from my eyes, thinking back to her prayers for me, at least until she and Penny went crazy and forgot who they were.

I warned you.

My poor Lela! Where the hell is Shirley?!

I curve down the bend of Highway 2 before it bends back northward onto Tom Foley Memorial Parkway and back to I-90. She's just a few short minutes away now.

An unlisted number rings my phone. I don't dare answer it. I know better. It's distracting.

Horns blare at me as I dodge and weave my way through early afternoon traffic, screaming east to get my little girl.

Before too long, I'm only minutes away, rushing south down Cedar Street, then South High Drive, about to bank left on West 33rd Avenue. I'm in the neighborhoods now. Pedestrians scramble out of my way, screaming obscenities.

Now your daughter will pay the price.

"Shirley, you better be there. God, please let Shirley be there with my little girl!" I rail, my voice bouncing around inside my car as frenetically as Moloch's threats bounce around my heart.

I'm here. Twenty-ish hellish minutes later, greatly reduced through my ripping through Spokane, I tear into the Sacajawea parking lot. It's nearly abandoned. I don't see Shirley's car anywhere. I pull up to the bus turnstile. There are no buses.

My heart is in my throat. My daughter is not here. I raise my hands to my hair and pull in agony, whirling around, desperate to find some trace of her. The world careens around me in a blue. A few school employees and straggler students meander about, wondering who I am. One of the employees barks obscenities at me for driving too fast.

No one is here. Lela certainly isn't. And with that, Moloch's voice goes for the killing stroke:

Goodbye.

That abominable, evil voice condemns me almost as much as I condemn myself for interfering. I have nowhere to go. I have no one to call and no one to trust.

I should've known better. I should have listened.

I interfered, and now Moloch has my little girl!

18: THE DESPERATION

The Past: ***Thursday August 13th 2020***

The calls don't stop ringing.

The school calls over and over – and texts me, *and* alerts me in the ParentSquare app – to alert me that Lela didn't show up today or yesterday, although I'm painfully aware of that fact

– as *well* as the fact that I'm the one who is solely responsible for her absences.

All I can do is excuse the absences and lie that she's sick. And as I do so, the knot in my stomach grows thicker.

I'm stuck in grief, sitting here in my apartment, stewing in misery, weeping for my little girl. I don't know where she is, I don't know if she's still alive, and all I can do is weep, wreathed in smoke and reeking of ash.

I'm waiting for something to galvanize me into action, but I'm immobilized and unsure where true north even is. My despondency is a palpable and felt ache – I did this. *I* did this to my little girl. Moloch warned me, and I did it anyway.

I stare at my gun, boring holes into it with my eyes, thinking of what lies beyond that fiery finish, wondering if Lela would even forgive me in the afterlife. Would any of them forgive me? I'd be listed with the criminals, and they'd say that I abandoned my own daughter. After all, what hope do I have that she's even alive? I've seen what Moloch can do. I've seen the twisted bodies and witnessed the strange symbols cut into the flesh of the murdered victims. The trigger is tempting, and it beckons to my misery, giving it a home.

But I can't. I just can't. That's not the solution. Even here in the thick of my loss, a thin shred of logic still prevails: that is *precisely* what Moloch would want me to do. Give up, abandon her, grieve, mourn and wail… and be stuck in despondent inaction forever. Unless, of course, I choose the one action he's demanded that I take.

Kill Aadhya.

He's got my little girl. Would I consider trading her for the life of Aadhya? How could I even do that? I never dreamed such a compromise would have ever reared its ugly head. But now, I have to admit… it doesn't look all that bad.

Doesn't look all that bad at all.

Desperate times call for desperate measures. I mean, those prisoners in there had their chance, right? If Moloch wants to use Airway Heights penitentiary as his hunting grounds as opposed to, say, a mall… or a church… or a *school*… isn't that preferred?

If I can only save the life of my little girl.

With a new resolve and starting with some slow, measured breaths, I grit my teeth and clench my ass. I stow my gun and rise, ready to do whatever I can to reclaim Lela.

Whatever I can.

I have no idea where to go. Elias said Seattle. So, I'm heading to Seattle. I still have the file that Gabriel gave me. Maybe that was his intent all along, to set me up on this wild goose chase.

Brickert, Kieran Icarus. I open the file. The police report has the gruesome photos inside of the victim that the Brickert's father killed just like Jones at Airway.

But it also has information on Kieran.

It doesn't take me long to find what I'm looking for.

16126 Midvale Ave North, Shoreline. It's a four and a half hour drive west across I-90 and then up I-5. My stupid ex-husband and I used to live in Tukwila, and though I had never really gotten up to Shoreline in north Seattle for anything memorable, I know full well where it is.

It might be a futile pursuit, but I can't go to the police; they won't believe me. I can't go to Airway; they'll know I interfered. I don't care what's happening back there with Elias… Gabriel… Moloch… or Airway. I just want my daughter back, and if it takes a long drive to find Aadhya, that seems just desperate enough to work.

Plenty of time to chew my nails, smoke, and get more pissed off the entire way. I'm currently suspended, and all I have is time to nurse a burgeoning grudge on the interstate. With Seattle traffic the way it is, that should help piss me off even further.

I can't believe what I'm doing, but I have to do it.

Before too long, I'm in my car and hurling myself westward across I-90, picking up several packs of smokes along the way. Marlboro Ultra-Light 100s and some Dr. Peppers will carry me through.

Hang on, Lela. Hang on, my baby girl.

I'm running out of cigarettes. I don't stop, though. It took long enough just stopping to get some gas; I'm not stopping again.

Concepción texts me a few times during the trip, asking if I'm okay. I fire back the cursory *fine, I'm driving* message. At one point she even calls, and though I don't want to, I tell her that Lela and I are on a little road trip and everything is fine. She wishes us well and I thank her, hang up, and then burst into tears of grief for my missing daughter.

But, at long last, through the fresh hell that is Seattle traffic, I'm finally in Shoreline, and I'm coming up on the neighborhood. The sun is setting, and the streetlights are on, thankfully. My stomach is getting tight, and I'm nervous. My hands are twitching from nerves and nicotine: a potent mix.

North 165th Street takes me down to Stone Avenue North, and then dumps me onto Midvale. I'm ten seconds away. There aren't many streetlights in this particular section of the neighborhood; I'll have to peer at the fronts of houses or at mailboxes to gather up the addresses.

16149 on the right. That means that even numbers are on the left. I turn to look. 16142. Next one's coming up. 16136. It should be one more…

16130 scrolls by. It's gotta be the next one.

I stop, right there in the middle of the road in the fading light, my car's engine almost as hot as I am inside. The sign on the house address doesn't lie; it was there long before my cruel fool's errand.

16124.

I frown. So, where the hell is 16126? The next one down would be a number *lower* than 16124. They don't ascend again… unless… this is a loop. *Ah!* I think to myself, *it must be on the other side of the loop.*

I find myself curving around. Even numbers are on the right side of the street now. I can barely make out the numbers. Some of the houses don't have them.

16106 I can see…

16112 Midvale…

My eyes flick to Apple Maps. *Stone Avenue North.* Where did Midvale go? So, when you go around the loop, it dumps you back onto Stone Avenue North, I guess. So, these houses don't even pertain. They're on the wrong street.

Maybe I missed it. I'm tired of driving. I exhale hotly, speeding up through this residential neighborhood to circle back around.

16149 on the right again. 16142 on the left. 16136. 16130…

I pause once more in the road just before the driveway to 16124. There *is* no 16126. Now I'm just pissed, having driven out here all this way. My car is filled with profanity and smoke; I've got to roll the window down to let some of the profanity out.

In the dimming light I can make out a white rambler with a green door. It sits about twenty feet back from the road past a short driveway on a slight incline and a tiny flower-edged front yard with large camellia bushes, and a few sparse trees. That's 16124.

Maybe at one time it was subdivided? Is that it? Or is there another house on the property? I don't want to trespass, but I need answers. *I need my daughter.*

With a sigh of resignation, I pull over on the side of the street and let the car cool down. I can at least go up and see if anyone is there and if they know anything about the house.

I grip the steering wheel tightly, whispering *please* to no one in particular. My lungs fill with staunch air and grim determination; I snuff out my cigarette and slowly pace up to the house. Before I'm even halfway up the drive, a youngish woman leans out of the front door with a baby on her hip.

"Can I help you?"

Her husband suddenly appears behind her. They look concerned.

"Uh, hi," I greet them, trying to be as innocuous and anodyne as possible. I don my most vapid voice, just to try to purge away the sadness I've been marinating in this entire drive, hoping against hope that they'll take me on in trust. "I'm from Spokane. You don't know me, my name's Tracie? I'm happy to show you my license." I snicker, uselessly.

They say nothing, just continue to watch me. The young man slowly ebbs his way in front of his wife, shielding her. He's clad in a blue Nike T-shirt and jeans, and looks like he's fresh out of the shower. A young couple. And by the looks of it, that's an infant baby *girl* on the wife's hip.

A baby girl. Just like my Lela.

"What can we help you with, Tracie?" the man says.

I keep walking, slowly, up to the door. "Yeah, well, that's just it, I'm not sure. I was looking for another address, but all I'm seeing is this one, 16124. I was trying to find 16126."

The young man looks at his wife curiously for a moment and then returns to me. "Um, I don't know, we're the one in between this one and that one," he says, motioning to the houses that flank his. "But we haven't lived here a long time, maybe it was different before we moved in." His eyes flicker around.

The house does look rather newer, but maybe it was remodeled. I stutter my way into a question. "Can- can I ask when you moved in here?"

The young man's brow furrows. His wife says his name, quietly, but I don't catch it. He holds up a finger as he gently pushes her further into the house and walks out a little closer to engage me.

"What's this about, Tracie?" he asks, suspiciously.

I take a deep sigh. I don't know what to tell him, I'm at my wit's end, and I'm out here on a thread that I might find *some* way to find this supposed Aadhya who let this damned spirit in that took my daughter. Something this young man probably won't even understand.

"Look, I, uh," I fidget, but I'm on the edge of tears. "You're not going to believe me, but I just drove all the way out here from Spokane trying to find a woman that might have some information on…" I end lamely, unsure if I can finish it.

"…on?" he presses.

Another deep breath. "On my daughter. She's… gone missing." My lip is twitching, and I can barely contain myself. "I, uh, I'm sorry," I offer with a sniff. "Well, I'm looking for a woman who might be able to help me. Do either of you happen to know an… Aadhya?"

He just studies me. "Aadhya?" he asks me, seemingly uncertain as to whether he pronounced it correctly. He scrunches his lips together and his eyes search his own surroundings. "I don't think I have." His wife agrees with him, quietly, and quickly, from behind. He shakes his head. "Sorry."

My tears come fast and strong now. As if a sluice has been lifted, my grief comes pouring out unrestrained. I drove all this way on a wish and a prayer, only to have my hope crushed into pulp at the end. I nod helplessly through my tears, wiping them away as best I can. "I understand. It's – it's okay.

I'm very sorry to trouble you." My chest is heaving from my sobs. "I'll just – I," I start, and then turn to leave.

"Michael," the woman behind him pleads, seemingly urging him to show some sympathy. He does.

"Ma'am, I'm sorry. If there's anything we could do, we sure would, Tracie."

I wave him off. "I believe you. It's fine." I'm almost to my car. "I'm so sorry to trouble you, uh…?" I turn back to him questioningly.

"Michael. Michael Brickert. This is my wife Steph."

My flesh crawls and my heart seizes up. I have no words; all I can do is stand there, frozen.

"You said Spokane?" he asks me, but my jaw has fallen to the ground. In the dim light the young man even looks like a friggin' relation of the Brickerts now, though he's slighter in build and with darker hair. *Holy crap…*

I nod, helplessly, rooted to the ground in horror, my eyes darting back and forth between Michael and Steph. I have no words.

"Michael, ask her…" his wife urges.

Michael looks back at Steph for reassurance; she nods, and then he turns back to me. The moon is out in full force now, shining down on the three of us, and I can barely make out their expressions anymore, but I'll never forget his next question as long as I live.

"This wouldn't have anything to do with the murders at the prison, would it?"

I can't answer. I can't do anything but blink the surprise out of my eyes. I can't even think.

"Are you looking for my mother, Julia? Is that who you're looking for?" he asks me, slowly moving toward me.

It would have everything *to do with the murders at the prison,* I think to myself, *and hell yes I'm looking for Julia!* My mind is racing, but my motor skills refuse to cooperate; they've collapsed entirely, and my tongue can no longer function. I'm stuck between wonder and fear and awe. My head is spinning, my body is reeling, and my heart is in my throat.

"Tracie?"

In the gathering darkness of Midvale Avenue North in Shoreline, a further blackness takes me, and I lose all sense of who, where, and why I am. I can just make out Michael lunging for me as I collapse to the pavement from exhaustion, nicotine, Dr. Pepper sugar crash, lack of sleep, and fear, mixed with gratitude and the slimmest fibers of hope.

The questions pile up within me.

Is this a young brother of the Brickerts?

Is Aadhya – *Julia* – here… somewhere?

Does Lela still have time?

Does she have a prayer?

The questions don't stop coming.

19: THE ANSWERS

*The Past: **Friday August 14th 2020***

It's quiet in my mind now.

I hear a mother slowly cooing her baby. Is it me? A dream… of course. It's me with baby Lela, and I remember her as an infant. My precious Lela, my daughter, only three weeks old. Just finished breastfeeding, and now it's time for the next nap. I cradle her in my arms, and the memories come.

The memories…

The memories?

Wait…

This isn't Lela, and I'm not me. That's another mama…

But the baby looks like me…

I shake my head to clear the fog that came over me, and realize that I'm in a strange place. My eyes pan around the room. It's late-slash-early, but I don't see a clock anywhere. The room crackles with a woodstove, burning quietly in the far corner opposite the front door. Someone has draped me with a light blanket, and I'm sprawled out on their couch.

Of course. The Brickert's little brother. Michael. And his wife Steph. Short for Stephanie, I presume. That must be her, off in some recess of the house cooing her daughter and putting her to sleep.

I sit up, slowly, quietly, so as not to disturb anyone. My watch makes its presence felt on my wrist, and I had forgotten that I had it on. I can read the numbers, faintly, in the dark.

12:53am.

How long have I been out? I wonder. I must have arrived here sometime between 6 and 7pm. The back of my head hurts, and something tugs on it painfully. I slowly raise my hand to feel around the area. There's a bandage on the back of my head, and my hair feels slightly damp underneath it. I must have fallen and bonked my head on the pavement when that tremendous revelation – who Michael is – flooded over me.

A water bottle has been deposited on the floor next to the couch, along with a container of hand sanitizer. I eagerly take a sip of the water and feverishly rub my hands with the hand sanitizing lotion. As I do I hear the gentle shushing of Steph in the next room, and some dim shuffling steps. Michael enters the front room. He's wearing a Covid mask.

"Oh, hey, good, you're awake… are you okay?" he asks me, sitting down on a loveseat stationed next to the couch that I'm on.

I'm groggy, but, yes, I'm okay. The bump doesn't feel like Mount Everest, and the only thing bruised is my ego, really. The knowledge that Michael is the Brickert twins' brother has settled, and in the dim, crackling firelight I can see traces of them on his face. But he's different. Maybe they look more like Aadhya – *Julia* – and not so much like their dad. Either that or Michael's dad must not be Kieran.

Uh-oh… that could only mean that Julia cheated on Kieran, because she must have been pregnant with Michael when she took those boys to the carnival…

I decide to stuff my suspicions for now, and just allow it to come out in conversation, if it will.

"I… think I'm okay. Do I have you to thank for this?" I ask, pointing to the back of my head. He nods.

"You took a pretty nasty spill when you fainted."

"Fainted. Wow."

"Never faint before?"

"Only every time I see Brad Pitt," I jest, and then take a swig of the bottled water. Michael chuckles.

"Your daughter is beautiful," I whisper to him, and his face lights up.

"Thank you. She's our first. Our pride and joy. Her name's Addison. A month old."

"Addison. I like that," I say, reaching up to adjust the bandage as it tugs on my hair, flinching a bit.

"I should check that. You've been out for a few hours; we should change the dressing."

"Are you a nurse?"

"Steph is," he beams. "A good one too. But she's taught me a bit about bandaging up strange wayfarers from Spokane."

My turn to chuckle. "Get a lot of those, do you?"

"No, not really," he says, rising and approaching me, shifting behind me. "Actually, it still looks good. It wasn't a big wound. Steph helped me get you into the house. We had a feeling you wouldn't want us calling 9-1-1."

"Oh?"

"Well, given what you said about-"

He stops, and pulls away from me, sitting back down in the loveseat with his hands up in helplessness. I just stare at him, studying him there in the quiet of the dark. I can't resist. I drove all this way, and I just have to know.

"How old are you, Michael, can I ask?"

"25."

"And… was your mother… Julia?"

He clenches his lips, and I can see it through his mask. His jaw takes on a pronounced outline beyond his ear strings. "She was. She was named that once, yes. But then she went back into all that Hindu stuff, and, well, it sounds like you already know the rest of the story."

"How do you know that?"

"Don't ask me… I don't know how, I could just tell." He takes a deep sigh and blows it out hot and slow, watching me with his eyebrows up. "No one would just drive all the way out from Spokane on the coattails of prison murders looking for their daughter unless they were intimately connected to what's going on." He gazes straight into my eyes. "Intimately connected to Gabriel and Elias."

I sigh, and avert his gaze.

"So, it is true," he says. It's not a question.

"It's true," I concede, and a hush falls over us.

"I'm sorry," he finally ventures. "Sorry about all of it. Including your daughter. Steph and I will help in whatever way we can."

As if on cue, Steph walks into the room, slipping on a mask as she sits down with us. Good timing – there had been no further noise from what I'm guessing is the nursery around the corner. Momentarily I feel bad that I didn't bring a mask.

"Hello, Tracie," she says, and plops down on the recliner next to Michael. They give each other a quick peck. "She's down," Steph whispers.

"Nice work," Michael congratulates her. Steph turns to me with an exhausted smile on her face.

"Started at 8:15. And then again at 9:03, 9:38, 9:42, 10:47, 12:02, and finally at 12:37." She rolls her eyes.

"I've definitely been there," I acknowledge. "Lela was tough to get to sleep as an infant too." Memories of the constant wakeups and late-night-slash-early-morning feedings tumble through my mind. "My daughter was the exact same way."

Steph frowns. "*Is* the exact same way, you mean."

I see what she means, and I appreciate it, but it's not the same. "Well, yes, I suppose so." I look them squarely in the eyes. "Yes, she's still alive. I have to believe that." They clench their lips and nod in belief with me. I take a moment to let it sink in, even in my own heart. "I just meant it was a long time ago. She's 12 now." I bite my lip, thinking about our last exchange only three days ago; I was there, but I wasn't even really there for her. I hate myself for that. If only I could snuggle with her and just listen to her, undistracted.

They watch me in silence.

"You'll find her, Tracie," Steph encourages me.

"Thank you," I whisper, but the darkness of the room swallows my words and digests them in silence. The heaviness of pending questions from both of us presses down on us with palpable weight. An insufferable curiosity is gnawing at all three of us. Who will start?

They do.

"Tracie," Steph asks, "what do you know about what's happening in Spokane?"

I shake my head. Here goes.

"I know about all of it. I'm a guard at Airway Heights."

Steph gasps. Michael's jaw drops out of his mask. "Are you serious?" she asks, drawing out the last word. I nod. "So, you've been there during all of this? And- and you know Gabriel? And Elias?"

I nod once more, sadly.

"What… what can you tell us?" Michael asks.

I take a deep breath. "Only that the two of them are… *bound*, somehow, to this thing that is happening. You might think I'm crazy if I tell you. But it's-"

"No, we won't," they both say, sitting up, nearly in unison. I eyeball each of them in surprise. Clearly, they know more than they're letting on.

"Well," I start slowly, "what can you tell me about Julia? About- your mother, Michael?"

Michael appears to visibly stiffen somewhat. His eyes flick down the corridor for a moment, as if he's not wanting his infant daughter to hear any of this. *Like she'd understand...* I think to myself.

Michael swallows. "I only know what my brothers told me. We were separated. When their dad died, a lot of things changed in their lives. I was only a baby. I was born in 1996. But they'd already been placed in foster homes because their dad had died, and she kind of – went crazy. I was an orphan and bounced around in the foster system.

"Their dad – *man*," he stops. "He was almost as crazy as my mom was back then. He actually has a record: probable cause arrest for a murder. They couldn't find enough evidence to convict him, though."

The murder that looked like Jones', I think. *The police report that Elias handed me about the copycat killing.*

"I think he was the bad guy all along. I think he had a demon in him. And unfortunately, because my mom started all the Hindu stuff she did, she angered it – or got too close to it – or something. I think it was there, all along, lurking, waiting for an opportunity to come in and take him over. But his kids – my stepbrothers – they were even weirder.

"I only really met them – well, *Gabriel*, to be precise – when I was six. They're eight years older than me, so he would have been 14 at the time. I don't remember much of it; it was a social worker meeting and some kind of attempt at connecting families, but it didn't work out. All I really remember is Gabriel was really creepy, but he was the only one who did the talking. Elias didn't say anything; he was just kind of off in a corner by himself."

I watch him unravel this backstory with grim fascination and intrigue. "So, you never really got to know him?"

"I never really got to know *either* of them. And, truthfully, after meeting and talking with Gabriel, I didn't really want to. They had these strange – *markings* – on their skin…"

"I know them well," I interrupt, nodding. "I've seen them."

He continues. "Well, then you know that Gabriel had more than Elias, and his could, well, *do* things." My mind instantly goes back to that strange tattoo. My head seems to shake 'no' of its own accord, as I heave a sigh. "Our mom did that. She carved the symbols into them. At the-"

"Carnival," I finish for him.

His look of recognition – and Steph's quick glance up at him in confirmation – tell both of them that I'm no flake; that I've truly been party to their story. "That's right. The carnival."

"The day their dad died."

Michael nods. "Well, *died* is one way of looking at it." He purses his lips.

"You think *she* killed him?" I tilt my head, remembering what Elias said about suspecting Gabriel as their father's killer.

He shakes his head. "I don't know what I think anymore. My own dad is still alive, but she messed him up pretty good. She's not well. In her head. From everything she got herself into, she just became… sick," he finishes, sadly. His hands are held out, almost pleading to me to make it better.

He's lived with this all his life, poor kid. "She was never well after her daughter died."

"Her daughter?" I tilt my head.

"Yeah. The twins are actually triplets, she told me once, but their sister died in childbirth. They never knew her and mom didn't talk about her much. But it crushed her and she kind of started to unravel at that point." That's bizarre. I hadn't known that; there was nothing in Elias' file about this. Michael continues.

"Anyway, I joined up in the military, but it didn't work out. I work up at the Trader Joe's now, up on 175th. Steph and I got married last year and just had Addie. But I keep tabs on them, and Elias writes me sometimes." He gets up and retrieves a small log from a rack next to the woodstove, opening the Lopi and throwing it on, gently. Sparks and cinders fly. For a flash, I remember Elias' disintegrating body in that cell as he disappeared into blood…

"Elias writes you?"

"Oh yeah. I have a big case of his letters in the second bedroom, it's nearly overflowing," he nearly chuckles. "Gabriel, though – not a peep."

I have to interject here.

"Michael, what else do you know about Aadhya, and the whole ritual stuff? Gabriel told me about the carnival, about the incantations, about the spells she tried to cast, all that."

He clenches his lips. "Not much, I've heard of a few of the things she tried to do. It sounds like Gabriel tried to reproduce some of that, though. It all sounds too eerily familiar to what my mom said he did when he was young. About-"

He stops, stiffening, and his frightened eyes call out to me in the dark. I see them, faintly glistening, as he's unsure whether or not he wants to even say the name. He doesn't need to. I do it for him.

"About Moloch."

He swallows hard, and blinks, but says nothing. Steph takes a huge sigh behind him, her eyebrows pointing feebly upwards in the dark.

"I know about it," I assure them. "I've seen it."

"Inside the prison?" Michael asks me. "Did you see-"

"Yes," I interrupt him again. "I saw some of the murders. It's Moloch, definitely."

He appears deflated, and shakes his head. "So, it was all true. Gabriel did it again."

"Yes, he did," I answer. "He said that he did it to give Elias a break, this whole body-swapping nonsense, though it could just be a huge act that I-"

He looks back up at me, nearly glaring. "It's not an act," he says with complete conviction. "It's *not* an act," he repeats.

I watch him, waiting.

"He did it with Elias right in front of Michael as a little boy," Steph says, weakly, and she grasps his knee in support. "And he tried to do it *to* Michael."

I gasp. "Oh, Michael, how horrible. I'm sorry."

He waves me off. "It's fine. It didn't work, but I want to say he came close. In any event, I believe all of it. And everything I've heard about those murders… especially about the one guy they found in the closet, that guard? Their dad did that, Tracie."

"I know. I saw the police report."

"Yeah."

"Do you believe that your mother was at the center of those spells?"

He nods briskly. "Yes. Yes, I do. But I have to believe that she never intended to unleash any evil upon the world. I think that was just an accident. An accident that Gabriel found to his liking, and decided to try again."

He turns and gazes into Steph's eyes. "An accident that ushered in *Moloch*." Steph nods in saddened resignation. "And," he says, turning back to face me with sorrow, "took your little girl away from you."

The lump in my throat is pronounced and obvious. I feel it. "Yeah," is all I can muster for a while, staring at the fire. I return to meet their eyes momentarily, in the darkening room. The new log is crackling plenty, but outside it's pitch black.

"Michael, Moloch wants me to kill Aadhya."

He stares at me in surprise. Steph grips his knee harder; the bones of her knuckles pronounced in the firelight.

"Moloch took my daughter because I kept involving myself with Elias and Gabriel. Elias said that Moloch takes over Elias' sleeping body, and that's how he keeps getting back into that prison. And Gabriel told me that Aadhya – *Julia* – was still alive. I wouldn't believe it, except for the fact that Gabriel also told me she was alive in the Seattle area."

He stares at me with furrowed brows. "So that's it? You've come here to kill her. To get your daughter back."

The wind is sucked out of me, and my head drops to the floor. "I don't know, Michael. I just don't know. I'm not sure of anything anymore." At that, I reach behind my back and pull out my Sig Sauer, slowly, staring at it.

Steph stiffens, and Michael reflexively stands to his feet, bracing, and shielding his wife behind him.

"It's the one way I can get Lela back," I whisper. "But that doesn't mean that I'm going to do it. Moloch is a killer."

I slowly stand, pace over to Michael, meet his eyes, and turn the chamber toward myself, handle extended outward toward him, placing it in his hands.

"I'm no killer," I breathe.

He swallows hard, and I can hear him pant through his mask as I return to sit down once more. I rest my head in my hands, my fingers threading my jumbled hair. I turn my eyes to the amber licks of flame and am lost in thought.

Michael sheepishly places the gun on a side table, looking at it with distaste, almost as if a memory from the armed forces troubles him. Maybe he just couldn't handle a weapon there. I don't know.

"Julia is my mother," he says. "She doesn't sleep. She never sleeps," he adds, as I watch him carefully. "She takes medicine intentionally, so that she *doesn't* sleep. If she goes to sleep…" he finishes, his throat catching, his eyes ringed with fear. "Tracie," he continues fitfully, "this house- it… it *used* to be 16126. We had to petition the county to change the house address because of what happened here. Because of what Julia did. Too many looky-loos and rubberneckers."

I'm just watching him as it all comes out.

He licks his lips nervously, explaining in greater detail and in quicker succession, almost like penance: it's as if he's trying to make peace with his own past. "But – again, my mom can't sleep. If she goes to sleep, she says Moloch will kill her. It's just that – that lack of sleep did things to her brain, and she's… crazy." My hands slip from my mouth. Can it be? I see where this is going. "She cast a spell over herself. Some… crazy incantation from that journal of hers. To keep herself awake, just this side of sleep. She technically died. We had her death certified, even. October 12th, 2003."

"But – how is that even possible?" I pry.

He shrugs. "We're dealing with the paranormal here, Tracie. I don't understand it; I don't expect you or anyone else to, either." Michael's eyes flick down the hall once more.

And now I know. I slowly cock my head down the hall where he glanced, and the truth slowly rolls over me.

Julia Rosetta Brickert is in this very house. Right now. Right down the hall from where we sit.

I slowly rise, and then I find myself running to her.

Steph screams "Stop!"

The baby wakes and cries out.

Michael yells something and tells me he'll shoot. I hear him retrieve my gun. That distinct sound of the *snick-chick* as it's being cocked. I can feel it trained on me as I rush down the hall. They follow me.

There are only three doors. I'm frantically scanning them all over. I can clearly make out the nursery: the door is open and there's white noise and a dim baby light filtering out into the hall.

Another door, ajar: clearly a bathroom.

One final door. It's shut.

I burst inside the room before they can stop me.

They're still shouting. But Steph has split off and scooped up Addie, retreating to the other end of the house to their master bedroom with her.

It's just me. And Michael.

And Aadhya.

I'm panting, standing over her in her bed, with her IV tube and medical equipment stationed nearby.

Those eyes. They stare out at me. They're looking *through* me.

Michael is right behind me, and I can practically feel the gun pointed straight at my back as he shouts at me, muffled through his mask.

There she is. A withered corpse of a woman, wrinkled beyond repair, eye sockets stretched overlong and ringed with fatigue. Thin wisps of her hair trail back down off her skeletal cranium into a single makeshift pigtail. Her bony, withered figure lies there, inert, mouth agape and breathing heavy yet silently. She looks roughly eighty… either that's her actual age or dealing with the paranormal has exacted a heavy toll on her flimsy humanity. She literally looks like death warmed over.

Michael pleads with me.

I'm ex-military. All it would take is a quick duck and back kick and I would send him sprawling. He didn't seem confident with a gun anyway. All I have to do is immobilize him and then shut and lock the door, and Aadhya would be all mine.

To smother. To strangle. To beat to a bloody pulp.

Then… I would have Lela back.

Wouldn't I? Could I take Moloch at his word that my daughter would be returned?

I'm panting, and my chest is heaving up and down as I stare at her, pondering my options. The tears come hot and thick as my eyes dart around the room, scanning her lifeless yet still-clinging soul, covered over with blanket upon blanket, her eyes still fixed upon me.

From somewhere at the other end of the house, Steph is screaming over the baby, yelling something to Michael. It's unintelligible over Michael's repeated threats for me to back off or he'll shoot. He repeats his command.

My daughter. My sweet Lela. She's within reach. I don't know how Moloch would even know, but surely, he *would* know, wouldn't he? He would know if I killed Julia Brickert for him.

Killed *Aadhya.*

My leg flexes along with my abs as I prepare to whirl around and back-kick him, sending him sprawling. My fingers flinch and then flex. I'm gathering my breath as my eyes peer to the side of myself, undetectable by him. I'm ready to make my move as Michael threatens once more and begins a solemn countdown.

Five... he groans.

Wait...

Something in the back of my mind stops me. Something Gabriel said to me.

Four...

All it would take is one swift kick. But didn't Gabriel say something about a- No! It was Elias speaking. Wasn't it? Or was it Moloch *through* Elias? All it would take is two seconds to break her neck, and I remember my training! I could do it, easily enough!

Three...

Elias' words come rushing back to me. *But you will find her and kill her before she can conduct the ritual that will banish Moloch.* If she's still alive – even barely – then she can conduct that ritual to banish Moloch!

Two…

She could do it! I don't know how, but she could do it! Right? *Right?!*

Michael's fingers flex. I can practically hear his knuckles crack. He's preparing to fire.

One…

"Stop! Michael, stop. Please." I slowly raise my hands in surrender, moving away from Aadhya, my face streaming with tears, my breath coming in thick, desperate heaves.

Lela's face appears in my mind's eye, in a blur coalescing into clarity. She's smiling. As a fading wish, or in approval of my decision to back off? All I can do is hope I learn the truth one day…

I slide over to the wall and slump down in a heap, bawling uncontrollably.

Michael is breathing erratically, grunting and swallowing in gulps. Afraid. I can hear him relax and back against the doorframe, watching me, still on sentry.

And then I look up and see her. She's *smiling* at me. Her lips are thin and frail, pressed together into a narrow curve that defies death, but those sunken eyes have now taken on a dim twinkle in the dark of the room, and her soul reaches out to me. If she's alive, then perhaps there's still hope for her to pronounce this incantation… perform this ritual… whatever, to stop Moloch.

She should be dead. She was *declared* dead. By all rights she *should* be dead now. But she's not dead. And certainly not by my hand.

My own words come back to me.

I- I'm no killer. I can't kill anyone. Please.

I can see Lela, but she's out of reach. At least for now. Moloch still has her. And Julia still lives. And Michael is still ready to shoot me.

I was *this* close to doing his bidding and receiving my daughter back. But I'm not ready to kill. That's someone else's pleasure and desire.

Not mine.

I'm no Moloch. And yet I was *this* close to becoming like him, as if he had body-swapped and was right here inside me. Controlling me, as he has done so many times with Gabriel and Elias… and perhaps others.

And with that realization, I bury my face in my hands there in that room, and just sob.

There is thunder in my heart now.

20: THE MOTHER

Present: **Wednesday, January 13th 2021**

I just sat and watched her.

Julia couldn't sleep – she was always awake from a spell that she cast over herself to forever shield herself from Moloch, so that he couldn't get inside her and kill her.

Michael had told me that, and as far-fetched as it was, it seemed to be true. I remember thinking, if Moloch could hop bodies and 'ride' people, and if he could body-swap asleep people and all of that, and *she* is the one who let him in, then it stands to reason that she would be his primary target.

She let him in; *she's* the one who could hand him his hat and show him the door.

There she lay, and there she stared at me with a kindly old smile: her wrinkled, taut face stretched in sweetness. It was early that morning, and, somehow, Steph had gotten Addison back to sleep. It was just Michael and me in there with the elderly undead form of Julia.

I just stared right back at her, transfixed as it were, consumed by awe over this woman who Moloch so wanted to be destroyed. The genesis of all of it. The cause of their ultimate downfall and the gatekeeper who foolishly left the gate open and ushered in the demon. I remember sitting there, warring within myself, wishing there was something I could do to free Lela from Moloch's clutches.

To ask her if she was still lucid enough to pronounce any kind of counterspell: this aged, decrepit witch confined to her outpatient hospital bed.

To just get answers from her. To find out the truth of the matter.

To ask her *why* she did all this in the first place.

To demand that she get my daughter back.

I remember watching her and wondering if she was even aware of Gabriel's sinister actions and demented Dr. Jekyll-slash-Mr. Hyde visage. Did she even know her child? Would she be at all surprised to learn about what he's done – what he's *doing* – both inside and outside Airway Heights Corrections Center?

Please, Julia, wake up, I remember thinking.

I take a long drag on my cigarette as I sit here in the cold of winter, staring out from my balcony onto a white-washed landscape which covers everything in quiet… even most of the sordid memories.

Except one.

Because then, to my amazement, it happened.

Slowly, to be sure, it happened, and Michael will always remember that day with me as well, though the miles and the memories separate us. He had been faithful to change her, to turn her over and avoid bedsores with the help of his nurse wife Steph, to secure medicines for her and keep her alive, to feed her… all of it.

She had been kept alive… for what? For me? For Lela? For the counterspell to banish Moloch?

We were about to find out.

21: THE PRAYER

*The Past: **Friday August 14th 2020***

It is a freaking miracle.

I will never understand faith, or God, or prayer, or Rosie, or any of that, fully. I've never really been a religious person. Concepción is a religious person. Rosie is a religious person. They both pray. Maybe I thought I'd just 'leave it to them.' I don't know. Do I believe in the afterlife? Well, I didn't – until all of this stuff began to happen to us.

But Michael tells me, here, today, that this must have been "all part of God's plan," whatever that means.

He's guarded, yes, and he still has my gun, but I think he senses, intrinsically, that there's no measurable need for it anymore. He knows I mean him – and Julia *and* his wife and infant daughter – no harm. He knows that I'm struggling, not insane. Crazy, not suicidal. Livid, not murderous.

And then it happens.

Michael had picked me up from the floor and ushered my bawling self back out into the living room. We're now sitting opposite each other. Steph finally comes out of the master bedroom with Addison, and she's breastfeeding her back in the nursery once again.

Michael and I are talking, softly. It begins with my sincere and heartfelt apology.

"I forgive you," he mumbles. He has taken off his mask, perhaps assuming that I was more of a physical threat than a Covid threat. That threat has been removed. After all, he still has my gun. "And I understand," he continues.

I scoff. "I don't know how you could."

"Easy," he answers. "You're desperate. I understand – more or less – what you're going through. I get it. I've been there too."

A flicker of his gun fear flashes through my mind. Time to venture a guess. "With the Army?"

He nods, slowly. "How'd you guess?"

"I saw how you regarded my gun. You're afraid."

Another slow nod. "Well, it's a long story. I'll spare you the details. An exercise gone wrong. It was supposed to be blanks, but one gun got through with live rounds. One dead by my hand. They chalked it up to an accident, but I still was the lucky recipient of a court-martial and a dishonorable discharge."

"How could you?"

"I was the one in charge of removing the live rounds. I thought I got all of them. And… I was desperate to prove myself in there. I was trying to get in and prove my mettle, I guess. I dunno. I… missed one."

"You think I'm desperate to prove myself?"

He looks uncertain. "No. No, it's not that. You're desperate to get your daughter back. That much is clear. And," he says, pausing for a deep breath, "I don't know how much my mom can help you with that, but I hope she can."

I study him for a moment. "You said you changed the address here. Because of the attention. Can I," I pause as well, "can I ask what happened?"

It must be the night of deep sighs, because there he goes again, glancing around in uncertainty, perhaps unsure of what he feels would be safe to tell me. He clears his throat.

"It all started with her affair. My last name technically is Randall, not Brickert. Mom must have a thing for WASP white dudes with muscles, because apparently my dad looked a lot like Gabriel and Elias' dad."

"Looked?"

His eyes squint. "He's dead now, too."

"I'm sorry, Michael."

Michael grits his teeth. "Anyway, there was that, first. The affair. Even in the 90's, it wasn't looked upon favorably.

But she's also pretty old, and my dad was pretty young. People felt she was robbing the cradle, really."

"How old is she?" I ask.

"Eighty-one." *I was right.* "Yeah, she was fifty-six then. My dad was only twenty. Pretty big gap."

"That *is* a big gap."

"Well, then, my stepdad – *their* dad – dies under mysterious circumstances, and it was grisly, apparently. I was just an infant. They were eight. My dad split as a result. He didn't want anything to do with it; it was on the news, sure enough, and all fingers pointed to Julia. And since she was going by 'Aadhya' at that time, everyone thought she was crazy. Except for the judge. Apparently, he thought she was sane enough to still maintain custody of me. Either that or Moloch got to him as well, to keep us together. I don't know and I don't care anymore."

"When did you see the twins again?" I ask, curious at the unraveling of his story… *all* the brothers' stories.

"2001," he answers. "That was the first time I told you about, when the social worker tried to get us all together. The twins had been bouncing around foster homes, and they had just kind of lost touch with mom. I think they were just going through all the typical teenage angst, all *GooGoo Dolls Iris* crap. But Gabriel: well, no foster family wanted to keep him. So, the social worker tried to put us all back together again. The judge figured it was the best thing for our family, and thought, with some counseling, we could be a cohesive family unit again or something." He scoffs and shakes his head. "Hindsight's always twenty-twenty, right? Foolish move."

"Why?"

"Because of Gabriel. He started getting into mom's journal and trying to practice all the stuff she was doing. He's the one who ushered in Moloch, remember. And he actually did, until mom did that counterspell thing. Elias never wanted any part of it."

I nod, connecting the dots. "So, it *is* possible. She did it once."

"She did," he confirms. "But not before Gabriel and Elias had successfully body swapped. She was able to do it, Tracie. She really was. But – and this is where I don't really know what happened – but I think she grew tired of doing the swapping thing, I dunno, maybe she was coming to her senses. I honestly think she sensed something on the periphery. I think back now, and I think she could actually *see* Moloch coming, ya know? Like she knew there was this presence lurking on the periphery, ready to spring in through the open conduit."

"How terrifying," I reply. "And that's when she closed it, when she bound him?"

Michael nods again. Steph returns from breastfeeding at that moment, but she doesn't give me any kind looks this time. She's tired, it's early, I brought a gun in here, and I did almost just kill her mother-in-law under her own roof. I'd be a wary and worn-out mama as well.

Steph sits down next to Michael once more, but this time she stretches out and eyes me darkly. "You okay, hon?" he asks her. She replies with a slow nod and a slow blink. I can tell she's exhausted.

"I'm – *sorry,* Steph," is all I can say. She sighs and nods her head. Not ready to forgive me. No problem. I completely understand.

Michael turns back to me. "Hmm? Oh yeah, right," he continues, remembering my question. "Well, not exactly. She just backed off. Like she had sobered up or something."

"Got it. But then Gabriel found a way through or something. He let him out intentionally?"

Michael nods, grimly. "Yeah. Unfortunately, yeah."

"Did you see what happened?"

He shakes his head. "No. I was never there when it happened. My dad sued for custody and won. That's when I lost touch with any of them. I was only really reconnected with my mom after I heard about Elias' crime, and found out that he was in the joint, and then learned that both of them lived in Spokane now. I had no idea she was still alive."

"When was that?" I feel like some snotty court reporter, peppering him with all these questions, making him squirm.

"Um, I think it was only a few years ago, right hon?" He turns to Steph for confirmation, and she nods her head. "We attended some of the trial proceedings."

"Why did you keep the name 'Brickert' if your dad got custody of you?" I ask him.

"Oh," he says, eyebrows flicking upward. "I didn't. The court changed it, but long after my dad died and I had nobody, I found out mom was still alive. I reconnected with her and had it changed back. Figured that would be easier on the system and records and taking care of her and everything. Not that I wanted to return to that name, of course, but it just made sense."

Makes perfectly bizarre sense, I think to myself.

A text suddenly comes through on my phone. It's Pastor Rosie. There have been more murders at Airway. She spares me the details, apologizing for the early morning text, but wanted to see if I was okay, and if I needed anything.

My heart goes out to everyone there in that prison. There have been dozens killed now, in gruesome fashion. It doesn't take a genius to know that how these new victims were all killed was no doubt equally as gory as the previous ones. Possibly even more so. I don't reply; I just hang my head.

"What is it?" Steph asks, dryly.

It takes me a second. Do I tell them? I *have* to tell them. It's Michael's brother, after all. "More… at Airway," is all I can breathe.

They both moan in their own fashion. Steph draws nearer to Michael. I watch the two of them snuggling close, and I'm reminded of my precious daughter, my Lela. She's out there somewhere, and I don't know where she is or what he's done with her. I can't explain how, but I know she's alive. And with that knowledge, the pressure of justice weighs on me.

There are guards and police in there. They weren't sentenced to imprisonment in Airway Heights. And even some of those inmates, committers of white-collar crimes: do they deserve to die as well? Is Lela's life worth more than all of them combined? Or even just one of them? Who decides?

Is any of this fair? Their blood collectively echoes in my mind, and the guilt of all of this weighs on me. I kill Julia, Moloch wins. Maybe I get my little girl back; but maybe I don't.

Moloch needs to be stopped; he really does… that much is clear, or this will never end, regardless of whether I get Lela back or not. I clench my jaw and grit my teeth.

Is this, as Michael says, *all part of God's plan?* Might Lela die so that others can live, and Moloch can be banished back to wherever he came from?

If there's even a chance that he can be banished…

Rosie's praying for me and for Lela. Surely that has to count for something. And Michael is a believer too.

Somehow, I summon up the courage and resolve to move forward honorably. I don't know how, but I've made my choice. "Michael," I whisper, "I'm not here to kill your mother. I swear to you. I just… I just want her to stop Moloch. But I'm afraid what that might mean for my daughter," I add, and my lips are quivering with grief. "I don't know where she is, and I don't know if I can save her. Would you," -here I stop, staring into the eyes of this stranger: so removed from me and yet such a connection to the Brickert brothers, and thus, to Moloch… but also to God- "would you please pray for me?"

He slowly nods. "Of course, Tracie." He musters up a faint smile and leans forward, clasping his hands. "Lord, this has hovered over our home and our lives for far too long. Gabriel did this, and now it's up to us to undo it. If my mom could only wake up – after all this time – and do what's needed of her. Do this incantation, or whatever it is, and put this demon back where he belongs. You can work miracles, Lord. We trust you. Would you please allow this miracle, and would you please protect Tracie's daughter and keep him from harming her?

"In Jesus' Name… amen," he finishes, quietly.

"Yes, Lord," Steph quickly adds with soft fervor, "Tracie's daughter Lela is innocent in this." At that, my heart pangs. "Please protect her and return her, Lord. Thank you."

And now I lose it, the tears flowing freely down my face. I try to form a sentence, but it doesn't come. Nothing comes, I'm in shock – or – something.

"Tracie?"

"N-nothing," I fumble. "I just – that was wonderful. Thank you for praying for my daughter." I muster a weak smile.

And that's when we all hear it – suddenly. Our heads flash down the hallway and then back to each other.

It's quiet, at first. Something nearly unnoticeable, a murmur, perhaps, but growing in volume.

A moan.

A whisper.

A faint cry or plea, and it's coming from down the hall.

Michael's eyes widen, as he turns to face Steph. They exchange glances, and then he returns to meet my gaze. He sizes me up for a moment, and then takes a deep breath.

"Well, that was quick. Seems like God cares for your daughter," he says, staring down the hall. I frown, confused, as he turns back to me. "She doesn't just wake up like this unless there's a reason. I think, uh," -here he glances once more, nervously, at his wife for confirmation- "I think it's pretty clear you're the reason."

I swallow nervously and heavily, instantly craving a smoke – but this is why I'm here. This is *exactly* why I'm here.

"Would you like to meet her?" he asks me pensively.

I slowly nod.

This is it.

Michael leads me, wordlessly, down the hall, leaving the gun with Steph. She gives him a worried look as he takes her hands for a moment and then slips off with me toward Julia's room. He nods to her. "It'll be okay."

Before I know it, we're back in the room with one Julia Rosetta Brickert. Instantly, her eyes study me, squinting in the dim light spilling over her from a soft end table light she's turned on, almost as if she recognizes me. Old people give you that look of recognition, searching their memory for some dim trace of a relic from their past, trying to associate it with you or something. I don't know.

Michael's words are ringing in my ears: "She doesn't just wake up like this unless there's a reason," and I wonder how many times they've talked with her, pled with her, having heard of all that Moloch is or might be doing, only to meet with glassy eyes and a vacant stare. I'm sure they've tried countless times to get her to do whatever spell it is that would banish him, only to hang their heads in dejected despair.

We walk in, quietly. Her eyes follow me the whole time, and there, in the dark, a quiet voice croaks out at me. "You're her, aren't you? The one that Elias loves."

I grunt, unsure how to respond to that. "Hello, Julia," is all I can muster.

"Aadhya," she corrects me with a smile and a rasp. "Hello, my Michael," she greets him, and he strides up to her, smooths her wispy hair back, and kisses her forehead.

"Are you okay? You need some water, mom?"

"No," she replies firmly. "But her daughter does," she says, pointing at me, her bony finger trembling in her old age. I frown. "Your daughter is thirsty," she clarifies.

"I- I don't," is all I can muster, confused. "Thirsty?"

Aadhya nods. "Yes. That place is dry, and she's alone. She needs water."

Oh, my goodness, she knows where my daughter is. My eyes are ringed with panic. "Where is she? *Where is she?!*" I ask, my voice raising in a yearning frenzy as I lurch toward her.

"Shhh! It's okay," she assures me, her pointing finger transforming into a tranquil palm extended outward at me. "Moloch has her. But you can get her back. He cannot kill the young," she says. "He has been forbidden."

Chills run through me at this bold declaration that I pin all my hopes to. I don't know how she knows this, and I don't care, but it's all I need to hear right now. She doesn't use as many words, but *your daughter is alive and will be safe* is what I hear in my heart.

"How can we- where-," I start, jumbled. "Do you know exactly where she is?" I plead.

Aadhya nods, peacefully. Her relaxed assurance settles me. "In the water tower. It's hot in there."

I find myself reaching for my phone…my fingers are twitching in nervous apprehension, and my phone falls from my grip and plummets to the floor.

"Easy, child," Aadhya assures me.

"Where! *Where* is the water tower?" I plead.

"Shadle Park," Aadhya breathes. "A steel reservoir, very distinctive. She's there. I would hurry, dear."

"Oh, my Go-" I scream in a desperate whirl as I rip myself out of there, dialing 911. *'I would hurry.' 'You don't need to tell me that!* In a flash, I'm back out in the living room. Before too long the operator asks me what my emergency is. I'm fumbling through words, reporting that my daughter has been kidnapped and is in the water tower at Shadle Park. The operator asks for my name and prods me with more annoying questions, but assures me that the police are on their way. I confirm my number is the best one for them to reach me at and beg that they keep her at the station in protective custody until I can get back. I'm crying through the whole thing.

The call is made. The police are on their way. I disassemble entirely and crumple to the floor in a heap. Steph approaches me, bending downward and placing a sympathetic hand on my shoulder. It's all I can do to keep my face dry. "Thank you," I whisper to her. "Thank you so much."

"You're welcome, Tracie," she returns empathetically.

I try to compose myself, fumbling with my phone and asking for their number so I can text them any updates once I leave. Steph gives me Michael's, and I send him a quick *Hi, it's Tracie* before venturing back into Aadhya's room. She's lying there staring at me as I approach, but her expression has changed. It's one of horror. She knows. *She knows* about Airway tonight.

"Now you must get back, Tracie," she says, and I startle at my own name. She knows that too. "They're waiting for you."

I tilt my head. "Who, Aadhya? *Who* is waiting for me? The police?"

"No," she shakes her head. "Gabriel and Elias are waiting for you," she croaks. "Both of them. I can do what is needed, but you must be with them in order for me to banish the unwanted presence. Elias must *not* sleep until the time is right.

"*Both* of them?" I cry out, and I hear baby Addison stir and cry out. I've been too loud, but I don't care. I have no idea where Gabriel is; no one does. How we're supposed to capture him and keep him contained in order to do this is beyond me.

Aadhya nods. "You must be physically present and touching both of them if I am to banish the unwanted presence. There is no other way."

The ecstatic joy of my daughter's rescue transforms to horror and grief. I have to race back to Spokane and convince someone – anyone – to believe me in this whole scenario, touching both of them while this frail old woman, near death, can sentence death. Upon Moloch. Upon all of these murders. Upon this whole chapter.

"You must hurry, Tracie. I will hold on as long as I can, but you must get there. Go."

At her word *go* I find myself racing – almost pulled and forced – out of their home. Not a word is said, but I turn and glance at Michael Brickert with gratitude. He says nothing, just grants me the courtesy of an empathetic smile.

Aadhya, however, has the look of an angel – or a saint – or something holy I've never witnessed before. Maybe she's been redeemed. Maybe she's renounced her witchcraft and what she's done. Maybe she's renounced… been washed clean... made new or… something. I don't know. All I know is I'm sent on my way, suddenly, speeding south on I-5 with the sweetness of an octogenarian's frail smile and hopes swelling over me and coursing through me.

I feel her. I *feel* Aadhya. I don't know how, but I feel her, and I know she'll know when I'm with her twins. I believe she'll do what's necessary.

I'm praying for a freaking miracle.

PART FOUR: THE CLOSURE

22: THE DELIVERANCE

Present: **Thursday, January 14th 2021**

She was going to be safe.

My heart was so afraid. If I knew then what I know now.

I remember screaming back over I-90, full of hope and fear, for a little over four hours. Due to an abundance of hope, I pulled over and bought some cigarettes on the way. And due to an abundance of fear, I pulled over and bought some cigarettes on the way. I chain-smoked the entire way home, and must have smelled like an ashtray when I pulled into the Spokane Police Department, I'm sure.

Despite being in and out of service along the I-90 corridor up in the mountains – *thanks a lot, Ma Bell* – I finally emerged on the east side of the Cascades to voice mails innumerable which had been left for me.

Voicemails that were the sweetest sound I ever heard.

The voice of my young daughter: safe, and in police custody in Spokane. She was rattled, scared, and hungry, but they were taking care of her. There had been no evidence of abuse; nothing suggesting anything untoward other than kidnapping, thank God. I called back and gave the case number to the Spokane PD receptionist, and they put me through to a Detective who was watching over her.

Thank God. *Thank you,* God. Really. That was the most anxious I had ever been in my entire life. It's one thing to know your child is missing and be consumed by fear; it's another thing to know your child has been found and be consumed by fear, afraid of some giant prank that would see her snatched away from you yet again.

Thankfully, however, I called her back and heard her sweet voice in my ear. I even intentionally swore just to make sure it was her. She promised to collect several dollars from me when I got home. I was so overjoyed I told her I'd write her a check for a cool million, which she assured me she would gladly accept. She even made sure I had the correct spelling of her name. *That girl...*

Thank you, Julia... Aadhya... whatever your name is.

I had texted Michael that they had found my daughter, and he and Steph rejoiced with me. He provided me an update that Julia was still lucid, but that we needed to act fast. A window might be closing soon.

I told him I would call him at the precise moment we had the twins together.

And that was that. Five months ago, I was screaming back east toward Spokane to the PD and a waiting detective there, as fast as I possibly could. I remember my head was so spinning that I nearly ran someone off the road, lost in thought. All the way home, I had absolutely no clue how I was going to convince someone to get Gabriel and Elias together for this whole swap-and-drop kerfuffle, but I was going to do my damnedest.

And then? Then it would be time for spaghetti and movie with my precious daughter.

Memories of what seems like a bygone era, in a completely different form, rush through me.

She was finally safe.

23: THE RALLYING

The Past: ***Friday August 14th 2020***

I will never let go.

My 12-year-old is in my embrace, and we're crying out every wet tear our bodies could possibly generate. I'm soaking her hair against my face, and she's whimpering against me.

She's traumatized, that much is clear; but at least she knows she's safe now, and at least I know it too.

A detective sits in the room with us, watching us both.

"Mom, you stink so bad," Lela complains, pressed against my breasts.

"Oh, I know, I know, hon, I'm sorry!" I giggle through my tears, my snot, and realize I must smell like either a tavern or a casino. "See how worried mama got? Oh, Lela, I'm so sorry. I'm so glad you're okay, honey."

"Me too," she says, quietly, almost dismissively. She doesn't want to talk about it, and that's okay. She's content just being held, and I'm content just holding her.

But – as much as it pains me to do so, I know that it has to come to an end.

"Lela," I tell her, "this isn't over, honey."

Her face scowls, and her eyebrows raise. "What?"

"It's not over yet. The man who took you, do you remember what he looked like?"

She nods, slowly, tentatively.

"Good. Keep that face fresh in your mind, as hard as that is. I've got to talk to the detectives about this."

"Okaaaayyyy…" she says in typical juvenile fashion, but compounded by the fact that she's uncertain where any of this is going.

I turn to the detective sitting in here with us. At once, she brightens, as if she was surveilling us with a certain apathy prior; her mood shift is jarring, and I can't put my finger on it. She's got a badge clipped to her belt, sporting a blue blazer despite the heat of midday.

"Detective," I start, "I need to talk with you privately. Is that okay?"

She slowly gazes over upon Lela. "Will you be okay, sweetheart?"

Lela nods, her eyes darting between the detective and me. "For how long, though?" The detective turns back to me, questioningly.

"It shouldn't take long," I assure both of them, and then turn back to my daughter. "I just need to talk to the detective about the man who did this."

With another concerned glance at Lela and one at me for equal measure, the detective rises, opens the door, and calls upon another female officer to escort Lela to another room where she can have additional comforts: games, beverages, a nice couch, et cetera. I assure my daughter that I'll be back as soon as I possibly can. She nods to me, and that's the last I see of her, being led off with the other officer.

The detective and I head back into the meeting room where Lela and I were. She starts first as we both sit across from each other at the tiny table within. "I'm Detective Gaskill." She pauses, studying me, and I study her. The first thing I notice is she's wearing way too much perfume. For a moment I remember our sweet Conchita's powerful fragrance. I try to dismiss it. But then she poses the question. "I have to ask, are you the same Tracie Vossler, the guard at Airway?"

"Yes," I breathe energetically. "That's why I need to talk to you. It's all about that, actually."

"There were more murders last night, weren't there?"

"Uh, yes, I heard… I'm not there though, I've been released on my own recognizance."

She furrows her brow. "Why?"

"It's a really long story, Detective. But I promise you – we're in the same line of work… keeping the peace and protecting the innocent. There are other guards – and inmates – whose lives are in danger."

"Okay, talk to me." She starts a tape recording.

I take a deep breath to cleanse the palette, hoping against hope that Gaskill has an open mind. "Okay. You're not gonna believe this, but here goes…"

I walk Gaskill through all of it.

Elias' incarceration. Gabriel's creepiness. Aadhya's long history. Kieran Brickert's alleged murder. The Airway Heights murders. The visit between the twins. Seeing the brothers in the forest. The strange phone call from Moloch. Rosie and Penny's unexpected attitude adjustment. The bizarre tattoo. The threats on Lela's life. The paranormal aspect. My trip to Shoreline. Michael Brickert. All of it.

She's a very patient lady, scribbling down notes and recording my testimony, circling back and verifying details here and there. I'd say she was keeping up pretty well, straight-faced and no BS as I laid it all out. But it was time to bring in the clincher, the exact reason why I was talking to her. I needed her help, badly.

"So that brings us to this morning," I say, nearly out of breath. "Aadhya says we must be physically present in order to isolate and banish Moloch. We have to be right there with both of them, subdue them, and actually, physically touch them. That's the only way Moloch can be banished. I *know* all of this sounds absurd, but I believe her one hundred percent. She's the one who pointed out where Lela was, after all. She knew!" I finish, holding my hands up.

Gaskill is silent for a moment, thinking over everything she's heard. She lays her pencil down, finally, and stares off into space for a moment, eventually clasping her hands in front of her and staring at me over her knuckles.

"Here's the thing, Ms. Vossler," she begins. "I looked you up in the system when we found your little girl? It's protocol." I nod. "I just wanted to make sure it was really you. The Deputy Warden doesn't speak too highly of you right now. And neither do some of the staff there, a, uh," -here she opens the file she has set on the table under her notepad- "Dr. Penelope Eggers and Pastor Rosie Campion?" She looks at me. "Sounds like you might have gotten yourself a bit more involved than you intended? Does any of that sound familiar?"

Gaskill continues staring at me as I deflate. The hope of her helping me viscerally slips away from me. "I've been hearing some pretty strange stuff, scary crap, actually. There was a shower-room massacre. Now, I've never been inside Airway, but the guys from our department that have been stationed over there? They're on leave now. They're traumatized, Tracie. Every inmate in that shower was suddenly synchronized, moving like… puppets on the same string, they said. All of 'em – bludgeoned with some kind of club and the water turned to scalding on 'em. Their bodies were bubbled over and peeling when they found them.

"And then there was the conjugal visit – some guy's wife flipped out on her inmate husband in minimum custody there while they were doing the deed; stabbed the crap out of him, and then slit her own throat. Now, why would she do that? They're still cleaning up the blood. That poor dude was just wanting to connect with his wife."

She pauses, taking a deep breath and staring holes into me. "Now, all of this sounds far-fetched, sure – I'll give you that. No mistake. But when I talked with the doc and the pastor there – and your Deputy Warden, they don't want to talk about no Tracie Vossler. Now, why do you think that might be, hmm?" she finishes.

I shake my head, the butterflies in my stomach flying now into every system in my body. "I don't have the foggiest clue," is all I can mumble. "All I know is I'm telling you the truth, and I need your help. Why don't you talk to Caleb Canton, the Supe? He trusts me. He would believe me."

"Canton is still on leave."

I sigh, exasperated. "Yes, I *know* he's on leave. I'm just saying that he would believe me. He knows I'm no flake. Can you talk to him?"

She doesn't answer me. "Why were you released on your own recognizance, Ms. Vossler?"

My chances of getting help are circling the drain, and I see it. I'm starting to get hot under the collar. I don't like this over-perfumed powderpuff Detective anymore, and she's pissing me off. "Because of the reason," I say, sarcastically.

"The reason?" Gaskill asks.

"Yeah. *Pick* one. How the hell should I know? All I know is that I've been caught up in the middle of all of this, and my daughter nearly paid for it! Now you're eyeballing me like *I'm* the bad guy?" My voice is rising, and I pound my fist on the table.

Gaskill sits back and puts her hands up. "Whoa now, just calm down, Tracie. No one here is calling you a criminal."

"Oh, but in *Airway* they are? Is that what you're saying? So that makes it true?"

"I'm not saying that at all. But, from the report provided by the two ladies at Airway, isn't it possible you may have gotten a little close to one or both of these twin brothers, and now you're just trying to cover your bases by getting one or both of them in trouble so that you're off the hook?"

I'm incredulous. Just simply incredulous. I shake my head, my tongue in my cheek, my hopes sinking down into my shoes. "We're done here. I'll talk to someone else. I'll talk to Airway directly."

"We're not done here."

"Oh yes, we are!" I shout. "You have no idea what I've been through, and how I've – and now my daughter as well! – been jerked around by these guys. I'm telling you they're dangerous" -here the door opens and in walks another officer, hearing the commotion- "and you've got to do something!"

"We'll do something, certainly," Gaskill says. She looks up at the male officer. "Is her daughter secure?" He nods. "Good. Stand up please, Ms. Vossler." Gaskill rises. My heart is in my throat. I know where this is going. I'm desperate. *Desperate!* And these people were supposed to help me!

I shake my head, grunt, and do as she asks.

"Turn around, please, Ms. Vossler."

"You're making a big mistake," I say, and in that moment I'm Elias, before myself and Warden Canton back there at Airway. I don't know if I'm issuing a warning or a threat, but I know what I *want* to issue.

"We'll see," Gaskill says, and I hear the cuffs come out. "Tracie Vossler," she starts, "you're under arrest. Please put your hands behind your back."

I continue shaking my head in disbelief, and begin to fill my lungs with hot, angry air.

Air that controls me. That fuels me.

Air that expands my lungs for the running this marine is about to do.

Air that equips me to get to where I need to go in a hurry, and set things right.

I'm tired, pissed, and running out of time. Lela is safe, that's all I know or care about, and they'll keep her safe. That's all I need to know now.

The cuffs go on, but they aren't even successful in fully clasping one over a single wrist. My training kicks in, and I focus. I'm suddenly assaulting a police officer. The male officer realizes instantly that I'm trying to escape, and he goes for a chokehold.

I shift to my left, suddenly, scooping my right leg and planting it behind him. Gaskill is shouting something, reaching for her gun. I wrap my right arm around both of his legs and knock his knees out from under him, lifting him and body slamming him to the hard granite floor.

The relatively silent act of his immobilization is deafening, drowned out in the immediacy of it all: only grunts and wheezes as I cripple the unnamed male officer with a jab to the head, seizing his Beretta. In the commotion, the desk is bumped around and flies backward, knocking the gun loose from Gaskill's hand as she shrieks. She yells at me. "Vossler, stop! You shouldn't mess with the police - this is not going to end well for you!"

I train his gun on her. "Give me your car keys and your badge. Right now. Do it!"

She scowls at me, fishing in her pocket as she glares at me. "Now *you're* making a big mistake. Where are you even going to go, Tracie?" I'm approaching her, slowly. Her hand extends out toward me with the keys. Gaskill is heavyset and covered in obnoxious perfume. She poses no threat to me whatsoever.

Nonetheless, I have to do what I have to do. I point her male officer's gun at her. "Turn around, Gaskill," I say.

Gaskill grimaces and sighs, shaking her own head. "You shouldn't mess with an ex-Marine," I take great delight in breathing at her, right before I wrap my right arm around her neck. "This is not going to end well for you."

She doesn't even fight as I pin my other arm directly between her head and mine behind her, pinching her neck in a sleeper hold and cutting off the circulation to her brain. In a moment, Gaskill collapses in a heap on the floor, and I take her gun as well, locking both of them in the office. Mercifully, everyone else is either down another hallway or out on patrol.

What am I doing what am I doing what am I doing, Tracie what the hell are you doing…

Doubly armed, I steal out the back door using her badge, and into the employee parking lot, repeatedly tapping her key fob. A Nissan Murano's lights flash thirty feet from me.

Within minutes, I'm racing toward Airway Heights.

I call Michael. Aadhya is still awake, and they're changing and feeding her. For a woman certified as deceased, he says it's the most alive she's ever been. "Everything going okay over there?" he asks me.

"Uh, *sure,*" I say, checking my rearview mirror for pursuing squad vehicles. None yet. It's only a twenty minute drive from the PD to Airway Heights. "I'll call you back. I'm almost to Airway. Thanks, Michael."

"You're welcome," he says, and hangs up.

Various visions of ensuing events flicker through my mind, unsure of how all of this will play out. All I know is that Gabriel is using Elias' body to kill, and Gabriel himself needs to be found and caught. All I know is that I'm alive; moving fast and furious now, intent on putting all of this behind us. All I know is that he won't mess with my little girl again, and that's the mama bear vengeance in me speaking loud and clear.

I don't know what trying to stop them will do to me – or Elias. In all of this, he seems to be the innocent one.

I wonder now if it was even him who committed that second-degree murder. My teeth grit as I silently indict Gabriel and lay the blame squarely on him in the bowels of my mind.

However it turns out, Elias could pay a steep price in this, just as steep as Gabriel could pay, and as *surely* as Moloch is about to pay.

I sigh deeply from my heart.
There's no escaping it.
I've got to let him go.

24: THE DIVERSION

The Past: ***Friday August 14th 2020***

I'm back at the prison, and night is coming.

Thankfully, my badge still works, and I scan myself in. *Good. They haven't deleted me in the system yet. I don't know that they would, but I consider this a stroke of fortune.*

I'm hurrying in from my car, scanning the parking lot and the road behind me. There aren't any sirens in pursuit, and that's good. I'll catch it hot when they catch me, I'm sure. For now, I'm still a free woman with a mission and a grudge.

It's 6:13pm, and the usual mayhem is underway, with an amplified police presence intermingling with the contingent of Airway guard staff. Some of these guys are unfamiliar to me as I walk in past Judy's desk. *Poor Judy.* Slaughtered by Moloch, just like the rest of them.

And somewhere in here is his host: Elias James Brickert. I've got to find wherever he is in here and tell them – make them understand – that he can *not* be allowed to sleep. Not for any reason whatsoever. That should lure Gabriel out of hiding. If he cannot body swap with Elias, then he doesn't have a hunting ground at Airway Heights anymore. And he'll come.

And then? We call in the heavy artillery with Julia, and have her do her thing. I don't even know how that's going to happen yet, but we'll cross that bridge when we get there.

Lela must be texting me nonstop, but I've turned off my phone. I can have them trace me, however that works. I've heard of cellphones pinging cell towers and revealing the transit location of their owners. Not gonna happen to me.

My poor Lela must be so worried though. She *has* to know in her heart – despite what she might have heard – that I'm doing this for her.

And everyone else.

Five minutes onsite, I run into my first check: Deputy Warden Whitmire.

"Dylan," I say, greeting him through a heavy pant.

"What the hell are you doing here?" he asks me, gruffly. He's always been a bit of an ass that way, even before he assumed the throne in Caleb's absence.

"Nice to see you too," I say, but without a shred of humor. "I need to talk with you."

"I'm a little busy here, Vossler," he groans. "And you're not supposed to be onsite per Dr. Eggers' orders."

"I understand that, sir. *Please.* I'm asking for five minutes of your time. That's all."

Dylan Whitmire looks me over, sizing me up for a coffin. I can read his contempt like an open book.

Finally, the Deputy Warden scoffs, shakes his head, and then trudges off gruffly. He literally takes but two steps, turns back sharply, and fires off an annoyed "Well, are you coming?"

I don't respond; I just fall in line behind him.

"It's all true. I promise you." My knees are bouncing in anticipation, hopeful to get this taken care of. I shared with him everything he questioned me about before, and all the subsequent details; however, I did take the convenience of omitting the *teency-weency* detail of my immobilizing two detectives at the Spokane Police Department. What he doesn't know won't kill him.

I check my watch on an impulse. It's 6:42pm; hardly 'five minutes' as I promised him, but color him intrigued: he's been patient and listened to everything I've walked him through, and with a surprising surplus of patience; far more than Detective Gaskill, at least.

I remember the first time he grilled me; he's more exhausted now, worn down from the murders that have happened on his watch, and he's definitely tired and perhaps open to exploring further options, since everything up until now has arguably failed.

"She actually *knew* where your daughter was, huh? In that Shadle Park water tower?"

"Yessir, she was. The police rescued Lela."

"Crazy. Well, I'm glad she's okay."

"Thank you, sir."

Whitmire rubs his face roughly, trying to purge out the rigor of the day. "So, you're saying," he grunts, "that if we get them both together, your Yogi witch lady-"

"*Yogic,*" I correct him.

"Whatever. She can, what, do this exorcism thing and then we get the bad guy out of 9254381?" he asks, referencing Elias by his number: an annoyingly impersonal habit he has that I suppose stems from his desire to distance himself from the likes of inmates. He's always had a bit of a snide and heartless regard for those in his charge here.

"Yessir, that's what I'm saying."

"And we have to keep 9254381 awake all this time until we've got his brother."

"That sounds right, sir."

He thinks to himself for a moment. "It does make sense," he finally huffs, rubbing his face. "All these murders happened after 9254381 went to sleep. How he kept getting out of custody in the hole and everything, though… friggin' mystery."

"Not when you factor in Moloch, sir."

He stares at me, gritting his teeth, and nodding. "*Moloch.* Good Lord…"

"I know what you mean, sir," I agree, tiredly.

At that moment, my Ring doorbell goes off. I glance down at my phone and suppress a gasp. Two officers are outside the door, and more are behind them.

Their guns are drawn.

Damnit. We don't have much time.

"Somewhere you need to be, Vossler?"

My attention is jerked back upward to him. "Huh? Uh, no, sir. Nothing. Just, uh, an Amazon package."

He studies me curiously. I can hear his analog clock ticking, each second sounding off like a detonation.

"Tell ya what," he says, finally, "I'm willing to engage you. I did talk with Caleb, and he trusts you. I think Eggers and Campion think you're a little nutty – but so are they. This thing has regrettably come to a head, and all I know is I'm tired of the damned body count, Vossler. I'm out of options."

I watch him: the man I expected help from the least, contrasting him heavily with Gaskill, and it fills me with hope once more. If I hadn't disabled the detectives, I wouldn't be sitting here right now; I'd be languishing in a cell, presumably right down the hall from my daughter, unable to do anything redemptive whatsoever.

Dylan Whitmire has redeemed me.

"So, here's what we'll do. We'll get Canterbury in here and we'll see what he can whip up."

Whitmire makes a quick phone call, and within five minutes Dr. Canterbury, the prison physician, is in the office with us. He's a nervous bumbler with thin wire-frame glasses.

"Well," Canterbury begins after a quick summary from Whitmore, in which he spared him the entire paranormal element of course, "we could administer Mr. Brickert sodium oxybate. It's an extended-release oral suspension prescription usually used to treat those with narcolepsy, cataplexy, or EDS."

"EDS?" Whitmire posits.

"Uh, Excessive Daytime Sleepiness," Canterbury responds, to which Whitmire, surprisingly, laughs.

"Sorry," the Deputy Warden replies. "You docs just love to acronymize everything." He chuckles again.

"Well, sir, I-"

"It's fine, it's fine," Whitmire says, waving him down. "You have my permission to proceed. We're in a bit of a time crunch, so if you can get going on this, that would be great. I presume you have an antagonist regimen to reverse it when and if we need to let 9254381 sleep once more?"

There's no 'if,' I think to myself. Elias must eventually be allowed to sleep, so that I can somehow connect Gabriel to him, and initiate the banishing under Aadhya's watch.

The doctor squints his eyes in confusion for a moment, but looks as though he realizes Whitmire was referring to Elias as his inmate number. "Yessir, yes, I do, but it's usually not necessary. GHB" -here Whitmire suppresses an effacing chuckle at yet another acronym, and Canterbury notices it – "has a half-life of 30-60 minutes. It will wear off on its own."

"Fine, fine. Please begin." He waves Canterbury off.

The doctor acknowledges and heads back out.

Whitmire shakes his head and just watches me.

"I hope you're right."

"I am right, sir, humbly speaking." I sit stone-faced before him, grim with sincerity.

"Well, alright then. Anything else?"

I take a breath, more for clearing out my own nervousness than for preparing some long-winded explanation.

"Actually, yes…"

He frowns.

"If this is going to work, I need you to lock down the prison – like, right now."

He frowns yet again, but this time with irritated, squinting eyes full of incredulity and suspicion.

The alarm sounds. The PA is blaring.

Whitmire is giving competing instructions over the com, instructing everyone to immediately head outside the prison walls, minus the regular guard patrol, which is to stay onsite. All he will say is that there's been a 'toxic containment anomaly' – which isn't entirely false given the paranormal element of all of this – and it's enough of a cover story to clear out the house of the police presence, lock down the inmates, and get Airway Heights secured.

And why should it not be? We're in the middle of a Covid pandemic, after all. No one wants it, and the police are moved out, leaving us to handle our own affairs; leaving us to contain our little 'toxic containment anomaly.' Fear is heightened right now anyway, and an outbreak of Covid within a penitentiary – an enclosed space from which there is no escape – could indeed be a death sentence for all involved, constituting more of a death toll than the murders themselves have. There's an invisible virus among us, creating fire, entering our bodies, taking control of us, weakening us, poisoning us, and it's all around us – sensed, certainly, but ravaging us unseen.

Just like Moloch.

I smile, pleasantly surprised that Deputy Warden Dylan Whitmire has swiftly become an unexpected ally and a valuable asset in this. I didn't expect him to believe my story. However, I seemingly, apparently, tapped the well of his intolerance for further exhaustion, and he's ready to set the stage to purge Moloch from Airway Heights forever.

A certain panic settles over Airway as the combined security forces intermingle and then separate, attempting to decipher the competing directives over the PA. It's working. Masks are handed out in plenty. The inmates report to their cells and are locked down. My fellow guards, employed here and answerable to the warden, stick around and hold down the fort, running to supplies for a small array of hazmat suits. The police, trusting that we've got things under control – as we, ahem, *usually* did in the days before Moloch – retreat outside the walls of Airway, along with their guns *and* their walkie-talkies, which could alert them to the fact that I'm in here. But they can no longer get in.

The doors are closed and sealed.

And now we wait.

"You better be right about this, Vossler," growls Whitmire. "Or it's going to be your ass *and* mine."

"Relax, Dylan," I say, dryly, watching the monitors and observing the police presence retreat outside the walls. "You have a nice ass; they'll respect it."

He cocks an eyebrow at me.

That's it.

We're trapped inside the prison, and night has come.

25: THE MEMORIES

Present: **Saturday, January 16th 2021**

It was almost too impossible to conceive of.

My head is in the clouds again, and I'm not exactly present with my Lela, but how could you blame me?

It all defies belief.

Everything that went down in August of 2021 is the stuff of legend… and myth. That Deputy Warden Dylan Whitmire should actually side with me and help me in this insane plot we concocted still blows me away.

He's gone now too, having been relieved of command by Caleb Canton, now restored to Warden. It was good to see Caleb come back, but he's answerable to the police, the Governor and the State of Washington. Though I think he would still trust me if I was there, he was incensed at how we handled everything and still doesn't know what to think.

All of it happened as it should, and I had an unforeseen ally that I couldn't have expected or foreseen. One that I desperately needed in order to shield me and keep this whole bizarre course of action moving forward along the avenue of fate and twisted imaginings.

There were just too many murders. Airway Heights had become a melting pot. It needed to be contained. Innocent men and women had died at the hands of a diabolical menace; an unstoppable demon, and our plot became the necessary evil to *purge* that evil: to put an end to what was going on inside those prison walls.

It's all history now. Not ancient history, but enough to allow us to breathe just a little better. Nonetheless, what happened would have totally been part of that crappy court reporter Mitch Landon's line of questioning, too, had I not tired of him and bolted out of there.

Such a sad turn, all of it. No one should die the deaths that those inmates and guards did. No one. That's why I did what I did.

Such a frustrating waste of lives.

Whitmire and I brought things to pass that otherwise would not have, and we shoulder the blame for both stopping the murderous rampage as well as setting in motion a chain of events that ended up costing us our good reputations and our identities.

We'll regret it with every fiber of our being for the rest of our lives. That much is true, and it always will be.

And now, out at ice cream with my dear Lela, I wonder how many times my daughter is at school, and the cruel teenage girls there murmur about her behind her back: "hey, look, it's the daughter of that prison guard freakshow." Poor Lela.

I didn't want Tracie Vossler to be on the news. I didn't want Lela to have to shoulder this, either. But now she has to.

I just wish all of this was finally over.

It's almost too unbearable to live with.

26: THE DECEPTION

The Past: ***Friday August 14th 2020***

Things are underway now.

Canterbury administered the whatever-he-called-it, and he reports that Inmate Number 9254381 is doing just fine. I breathe a sigh of relief. Denying Elias sleep is the only way to subdue Moloch and prevent Gabriel from channeling him into Airway Heights once more.

If I'm right, Gabriel will grow impatient, come out of hiding, and will come to the one place where he can connect with his brother physically and initiate the transfer.

And we'll be waiting for him.

I text Michael and let him know the time is near. I can feel it. Michael confirms Aadhya is still awake and conversant. She's been kept up to date on where we are, and she's actually channeling her energies – that's what she said – toward guiding Gabriel to us. I pray it works. We've staked a lot to him showing up, and the end feels near.

But now there are two new wrinkles.

One, Lela. It's probably a foregone conclusion now that I'm inside Airway, so there was little point to leaving my phone off. As with Concepción on my way back from Seattle, once I turn my phone on, a flood of texts come rolling in.

Mom.

Mom…?

MOM!

A litany of complaints; a tirade of worried suppositions on what's going to happen to me, a cavalcade of frustrated ramblings and lengthy voice mails dripping with teenage angst. My heart aches as I realize there's simply nothing I can to assuage her anguish or solve this for her in the immediacy of her need. I'm not even sure I'll be able to solve it at all.

But on and on they come in. She's right to be angry: she's been through hell and back, and now she's sitting at the police station in their custody, waiting, hoping against hope that she'll be able to get out soon. Myriad voice mails show up as well: from Lela, from Concepción…

…and from the police. They're looking for me. Gaskill calls and urges me to turn myself in and 'the consequences will be lessened.' I sneer at that. She appeals to me, as an ex-Marine, to drop the campaign and submit to reason. "This is going to end very badly for you," she threatens, and I simply smirk, remembering how she basically gave up and slumped to the floor in my sleeper hold. I feel zero remorse for having done what needed to be done.

For Whitmire and me, we've come out of hiding and are preparing to hold a conference with our own troops in the employee conference room. A few guards are stationed throughout to ensure that no inmate roams free, and of course, Canterbury is in medical with Elias. But Penny and Rosie are in here with us. Their panicked eyes stare out over their masks at me in surprise, but they vocalize nothing.

Rosie's eyes, however: they say something. They speak to me. I don't know what it is, but she pauses long enough to connect with me visually, and it's as if she's trying to communicate something. An arcane message somehow? A message of hope? Belief? There's a supernatural element to that woman, supernatural in its own right. She's in tune with the spiritual, and I feel it.

Regardless, I don't know what it is, but they and everyone else gathered here are absolutely shocked to see us out of hazmat suits, and thus, unprotected. Exclamations of dismay ring out from the crowd of them gathered here.

The guards are scared; we've purged the police presence for my own sake… but also because the police will never let

Gabriel get anywhere near Elias without firing on him. If that happens, Moloch is neither banished nor killed even if Gabriel is; he'll find a new host body and keep up his murderous rampage.

Dylan and I begin with assuring everyone that there's no toxic threat. Many of them are confused by this, and are reluctant to remove their hazmat suits, but as we have none and appear to be just fine, several take us on in trust and remove their suits, though they're still donning their Covid masks underneath. I suppose that gives them some modicum of comfort in the wake of this frightening sea change. It takes some convincing, because they don't like Dylan as much as they liked Caleb. But – something I said or did appealed to Dylan to trust me and side with me entirely. For that, I'm grateful, because his authority can sway his men, and it appears to be doing just that.

Many of them, beyond the lack of hazmat suit, are surprised to see me here at all. Rumors apparently have been flying – spread either initially by Dylan himself, or by the ever-charitable Dr. Penny and Pastor Rosie, that there's possibly a love tryst between myself and Elias, thus my being put on suspension. I did, after all, escort Elias back into the prison after being out there with him in the forest. Whatever.

"Here's the situation, folks," Whitmire begins. "Many of you are new here, and I know this is all kind of crazy. Bear with me. Bear with *us*," he insists, "but a lot of you have been here for a while and you know Guard Tracie Vossler here. She's been here for a while, and she's no flake."

I'm no flake. Thanks, Dylan. That's confidence inspiring.

"She's shared with me what's going on. What's *really* going on. Now, I wouldn't believe her had I not seen the footage myself. Much of it is inexplicable. Much of it is disturbing. And all of it is not something we've dealt with before, folks. As Deputy Warden in Caleb Canton's absence, I've been paying attention, and we've lost a lot of good men – and inmates. What I've seen on the surveillance tapes speaks to a paranormal aspect that is both frightening and hard to fight. It's made us desperate.

"And it's made Vossler, here, desperate." He motions to me. "The man behind all of this kidnapped her little girl." Various gasps. Whitmire calms them. "She's okay, thank God, and she's in police custody. But Vossler had to take certain, ahem, *measures*, to get out of police custody, and that's why we had to move them out of here. The only way to stop these murders is to stop the man responsible, and Vossler here knows how to do that."

"That's crap, Warden!" voices one of the newer guards. "Now we don't have any guns in here anymore. If it's this Brickert guy, then we need the police in here to shoot him once he starts going on a rampage, simple as that!"

Whitmire shuts him down quickly. "I understand your concern, Trejo, but we cannot just kill the man."

Trejo shakes his head. "No. No! Forget about due process for a minute, Warden – it's either him or us! And-"

The deep change in Whitmire's voice is astounding. "You're not listening to me, Guard! Sit down! Are you deaf? We kill Inmate Number 9254381 and these killings continue unabated! They *will* go on, even after he's *dead*!"

Trejo silences, confused, but curious enough to listen now. He does as he's told and sits down with a disgruntled sigh through his mask.

"Now *listen* to me. All of you! You need to have an open mind for what we're about to tell you. Those guys out there are just paid to do an unthinkable job. They'd kill our perp onsite without a second thought. If they do that, it's all over. We can't allow that to happen. That's why the PA announcement. That's why the diversion. We need to contain this internally.

"I'm gonna relinquish the floor to Miss Vossler here. She was close to Cathcart. And Big Shirley, God rest her soul," he adds, mournfully. My heart sinks: it's then that I learn that Shirley has died… somehow. That's a bomb. No wonder she wasn't outside Lela's school. "You're gonna have to open your mind and *listen*" -here he nearly glares at Trejo- "to everything she tells you, or you'll answer to me."

He silently gazes out at all of them, passing his eyes over the crowd sternly.

"Tracie?" Whitmire steps aside.

I take a deep breath, and step up. This is it. *You got this, Tracie.*

"Thanks everyone," I start. "All I can say is that it's true. Those of you who have been here throughout this whole thing – who saw the aftermath of McAllister's murder in the R Building, who saw the footage of Caleb's wife, who witnessed the shower scene, you know there's something bigger going on. Something that can't be stopped simply by firepower.

"I will tell you that Inmate Elias Brickert," -here I find myself stuttering a bit, as I've just painted crosshairs on his back- "is truly at the center of it all. But," I hold up a finger, "it's really not that simple. There's something else at play, and it's a much scarier element than what we can see. Brickert isn't alone in this. He has a twin brother. And that twin brother has been playing with fire."

As quickly as I can, I give them the encapsulated nutshell of all that has led up to today, including Julia's transformation to Aadhya, Gabriel's invoking Moloch, Elias' body-swapping, his cryptic visitation conversation with Gabriel, my encounters with Moloch, the kidnapping of my daughter, traveling to Shoreline, Aadhya's revelation of Lela's location, and how I busted out of police custody.

"I'm an ex-Marine," I say, somewhat sheepishly. "I don't give up easily, and I want to see this through. *Semper fi*," I add, as a lame afterthought, but one that I fully mean. There are proud glances coming from some of them now: doubtless they have also served in either the Marines or another branch, and they understand. "I want to make it clear though that at no time, did I have any kind of relationship with Elias Brickert or his brother. For whatever reason I've been wrapped up in this. *Yes,* I've found him attractive; that hardly constitutes conspiracy, however."

I catch Rosie's eyes staring out at me once more.

"But this, *being*, this Moloch guy, he can move in and out of people as he wishes, I think. Or he can influence people, or something. He can definitely move from Elias Brickert's brother Gabriel. That much is clear now. So, we've got to get him here, and we've got to initiate putting them both to sleep so we can do whatever it is we need to do to kick this demon to the curb. *He's* the one who is ultimately responsible for all the deaths that have happened here. Not Elias Brickert."

They watch me, sullenly, digesting all of this paranormal crap, unsure of what might be required of them, but seemingly incensed enough at the deaths of their colleagues that they're prepared to take a stand.

"So, what do you need from us?" asks another guard whose name I don't know.

Here's where it gets interesting and we find out how committed these guys are, I think to myself. I flash a concerned glance over at Whitmire.

"Well, first, we're gonna need some good actors," I say. The guard raises his eyebrows.

We watch on the monitor. I still can't believe the volunteers we got.

The man is an established guard at various prisons, and came up from Walla Walla. His name is Julian Perry, and he was all too willing to do a little acting.

And the other volunteer, the woman? None other than Dr. Penelope Eggers: she of the British brogue and fierce warnings about unrequited yearnings. I couldn't believe it when she raised her hand.

There they are now, stumbling, staggering, lumbering like drunken oxen into the front lobby of Airway, clutching their own throats, pretending to gag for air, clawing at the front windows of the Airway Heights lobby entrance, secured, unable to be opened from either side until this lockdown is over.

They do their part, feverishly coughing with eyes rolling back in their heads, caught in the middle of a performance that would rival Meryl Streep in *Sophie's Choice* or Robert DeNiro in *Raging Bull.* I shake my head in disbelief, but there they are, right there, with the police on the other side, watching with contorted expressions of agony.

It's enough of a convincing ruse to repel them back even further. *Something awful is really happening within Airway Heights*, their frightened expressions scream.

I'll never forget it. Right before Dr. Penny went out, through the muffle of her mask she turned to me. "This is all bollocks, you know. Pure codswallop," she added.

I chuckled. "You really are British, aren't you?"

"*Irretrievably*," she said, sternly. "But, we Brits know when to rise up and do the right thing. That – whatever it was – that came over Rosie and me a few days ago, I shall never be able to understand it nor explain it. It's a wee bit overly dramatic for this biddy," she added, exhaustedly. "Ergo, drama begets drama, and, as a former headlining actress in London's West End, I shall therefore do my part to put these oddities in their place." She nodded in her own confirmation to what she just said, and then practically pranced off to the front to begin her thespian *oeuvre*, her quintessential performance.

My eyes followed her with grim respect.

And there she is now: dear Penny, redeemed, giving the performance of her life, her chin dribbling with bubbling spit and froth, clutching at her own throat. Enough to convince them, along with Officer Perry's *prima donna* display, that things were *definitely* not right inside Airway, and that they should keep their distance.

They both collapse in a heap, their backs to the windows, lying on their sides as they've been told, so that they can still breathe. Dr. Penny even gives the security camera a fiendish *wink*.

"Alright, that's that. Let's hope they take the bait and know that it's not safe in here," Whitmire says. "Now what, Vossler? How do we get the brother in here?

"He'll come," I say. "He's trying even now. I know it. It's getting dark outside, Dylan. He'll come."

Whitmire takes a deep breath and exhales hotly.

There's a knock on the door of his office. We both turn. It's Rosie.

Her mask has been pulled down over her chin. "May I come in?" she asks, gently.

"Please," invites Whitmire. Rosie comes in, with her hands clasped at her waist. She sits next to me on the other side of Whitmire's desk, and offers a gracious smile. I briefly wondered if it's the first Rosie I met, or the second, confused one. But that smile is disarming and friendly, with no trace of delusion.

"Warden Whitmire," she begins. "Thank you for spearheading this. As a woman of faith, I'm troubled by all of this, and just wanted to come in and express that. You're dealing with a demonic element here, such as has not been seen inside these walls."

"Yes, that's true," he agrees.

"I just wanted to let you know that, as the pastor here, I've spoken to a few of the inmates, yes, but to many of the guards as well, old and new. They're nervous sir; on edge. They want to help, and they're going to do what's expected of them, but I wanted to make myself available to them for prayer, and to pray over everyone before, well," she fumbles for her words, "before you do the *whatever-it-is* that you're planning on doing with Mr. Brickert."

"That's totally fine with me, Pastor Rosie. You have leave to govern your duties however you see fit," he answers.

"Oh, it's not a duty," she asserts. "It's a pleasure and a calling," she says.

"Fine," Whitmire concedes.

"Anyway, I just wanted to make sure it was alright. I can set up post in the conference room or something."

"That works fine with me," Whitmire answers, and then his phone rings. "Would you excuse me?" he asks, holding up a palm. He answers the line. "Warden Whitmire," he greets. "Yes, that's right."

There's nothing further. No sound.

Except the sound of amazement painted all over his face.

I look at Rosie.

Rosie looks at me. We both look back to Whitmire. There's a long, drawn-out and uncomfortable silence with the dull rumble of someone imparting some information to him from the other end of that line. His eyes squint and his head momentarily shakes as he listens in disbelief. He's not liking what he's hearing, that much is clear.

"Could you – say that again?" he eventually asks. Silence. "And you're bringing him here?" Pause. "Well, as you may have heard, we're in the middle of a lockdown situation due to a toxic containment anomaly."

More silence.

"Alright then," he says. "Fine. We'll see you in thirty."

Whitmire hangs up the phone.

"Well, Pastor Rosie," he says, quietly, folding his hands over his desk. "It seems like your prayers might actually be needed more than I had at first thought."

I glance at Rosie. She tilts her head in confusion.

"That was Spokane PD. Apparently, Gabriel Brickert just surrendered. He gave a full confession and asked to be transferred to the prison for custody in exchange for information on the Airway Heights Corrections Center murderer." He raises his eyebrows. "They're doing it. He's on his way. And Tracie, they want you as exchange for him."

Aghast, I feverishly reach for my phone to text Michael Brickert. Aadhya *must* be awake for this! I don't care so much about them knowing my location; that was an inevitability. But them *wanting* me: yikes. We have to find a way around that.

But – Gabriel Brickert is coming here! Just like we thought. This can end tonight!

He is on his way here now.

27: THE REUNION

The Past: ***Friday August 14th 2020***

Elias is still awake.

The police are en route, with Gabriel in custody. It's only a 20 minute drive from Spokane to PD to Airway.

They're coming.

I'm now on the phone with Michael. He assures me that Aadhya will be ready. Thankfully, despite the hour, she's been lucid and alert all day. Almost as if she's waited for this very day through longsuffering patience and expectation.

With all of her Yogic stuff, I wonder if she's been given either premonitions, or the ability to see beyond the present and into the future.

I hope, in all of it, she sees a good outcome.

We'll soon know.

They're getting me ready in in a hazmat suit, preparing for the exchange. I can't believe it's come to this.

The police are five minutes away, and with them, they have in custody one Gabriel Titus Brickert.

The firstborn son of Aadhya.

Brother to Elias James Brickert.

Brother to deceased triplet sister.

Son to a murdered father.

Hindu ritual practitioner.

Mass Murderer!

I have no idea why the police would allow him to be transferred to Airway. It *is* a prison, after all, but they have holding cells there, and they're well aware of the 'outbreak' that happened today. I can only assume that he's working his limited magic on those around him, as he did with Rosie and Penny when they ushered me out of there. Or maybe the notion of exchanging him for me was enough to satisfy them, and they knew we'd want him.

However you slice it, it's clear: it's always been about what Moloch wants, and he has, so far, gotten what he wants. I'm sure he knew I was at Airway. I'm sure he told them rather than them pinging my phone. I scowl at the memory of my interactions with him, wondering what I'll do when I see him here again, but knowing in my heart the *precise* reason why he wants to come here.

He wants to be with Elias. He wants to get him asleep and then body swap with him. Why can't he just kill on his own? I don't know. Is Gabriel some kind of tainted conduit? Can the killings *only* be done through Elias?

As with so many other things, we're going to find out.

Our guys in the yellow hazmat suits are ready. So am I.

A black Spokane Police Department SUV arrives, threading its way through the busy parking lot, weaving between news vans, cop cars, and other vehicles belonging to staff here. It pulls right up to the front doors, and the double doors swing open.

We've got our own guys ready to keep up the act. Dear Penny and Julian have been extracted and removed from sight, 'placed in temporary medical examination' for the doctor. Our guys are joined by two of their own: two armed officers wearing green hazmat suits of their own. It's a colorful parade that greets Gabriel Brickert at the back of the van and then ushers him in.

The front doors unlock with a determined concussion and an annoyingly staccato buzz. Police run for cover, clearing out from the general vicinity of the front doors, in no mood to become infected during what should be a simple transfer.

Gabriel is himself cuffed and dressed in a green hazmat suit as well, all of them being under the belief that Airway truly is contaminated by Covid – or worse. Perhaps the police were all too willing to send this mass murderer directly into a tainted custody. Maybe a Covid death would be sufficient revenge against him, they must think.

Our guys spray him down with a vaporous mix that one of our guards whipped up in some manual pressure washers. It's a gaseous mix that resembles some form of decontaminant: enough of a visual to convince the rest of the police force to back off and give us a wide berth as the doors open.

There he is.

They wanted me as a trade. Well, so be it. The two hazmat-suited police escort Gabriel in after the spray-down, taking into custody one Tracie Vossler, ex-marine, mother to beloved Lela, outfitted in a hazmat suit, leading her outside to the same waiting SUV.

The exchange is made, and the doors are locked tight once more.

Here we go.

By now, I'm sure they've unmasked the female guard doubling as me in the hazmat suit. I don't know her. I've never met her; she's a transfer from another joint. But she sure took on a brave assignment. Maybe they don't know me by sight and will only be able to verify that it's not me once they get her back to the police station. Either way, those hazmat suits obscure our faces, and that comes in handy. I think for a moment, comically, of the notion of Lela, back at the station, curiously watching them unmask this strange woman and having Lela's face contort in lack of recognition and surprise.

Haha.

So, we get Gabriel, and they get nothing. Neener neener. And now, here come our two guards with their two police officers, escorting Gabriel further through the lobby into the admin offices. They're now out of sight of the parking lot.

Suddenly, Whitmire greets them from around a corner. The two guards recoil, surprised to see anyone out of a mask or hazmat suit. "Hey!" exclaims one of the cops.

In a flash of movement, our guys grab the two green hazmat-suited officers. "What the…" one of them exclaims, and puts up a fight. He's subdued by superior numbers, and they seize their guns and walkie-talkies from both of them. Another of our guys take their handcuff keys.

"What are you *doing*?" asks the other in a livid tone, but he's muzzled, and they tape his mouth shut. Both of them are dragged off to a side room as others corner and train their weapons on Gabriel. All of us are in so much trouble, it's not even funny. But we'd rather have human enemies familiar with justice than supernatural ones obsessed with 'recreation.'

They strip Gabriel of his hazmat suit.

There he is.

Gabriel. I look at him. The sonofabitch who kidnapped my daughter. His smug smirk says it all as we keep our guns on him, strip him of his hazmat suit, uncuffing him as they do so. He eyes me, and me only, in the entire exchange. "Greetings, Ms. Vossler," he once more hisses, eerily. Beyond a shadow of a doubt, I know it's him, standing there before us. They quickly re-cuff him. As they do so, he has a Tourette's twinge, and with that, I need no further confirmation that it's him.

I seize my moment; in a flash of movement, I'm on him, slugging him in the gut as all of the air leaves him and he doubles over. With a deft half-circle, my left elbow crashes down on top of his back and sends him tumbling straight to the floor, pinning his own cuffed hands beneath him. I'm panting and growling, towering over him.

"Vossler!" Whitmire cries. "Stop that *now!*" Fierce meaty hands grab me from behind. It's Dylan, and he pulls me away from Gabriel.

"Tracie, no!" cries another voice, and before I know it, Rosie has her hand on my chest, pushing me back and away from Gabriel.

Whitmire watches as our guards extract Gabriel from the floor, then he flashes an angry, final glance at me. "Let's go, quickly now," says Whitmire.

In tow, Dr. Penny and Rosie follow us further down long corridors to Medical, where Dr. Canterbury is waiting with Elias. The good doctor probably knows nothing of our sabotage, and has no idea what's coming. I wonder if Gabriel even has any idea. We leave behind two guards to watch the cops, but not before we tie them up and lock them in a supply closet for now. We're taking the guns with us, and keeping Gabriel in our crosshairs.

On the way, a squawk comes over the radio. The police are wanting an update from their officers who are now subdued.

"What do we tell them?" I ask Whitmire. His eyes search the corridors around him, unsure of what to say.

"All is well, transferring subject to medical, stand by please," he finally says, in the most pathetic disguised voice he could possibly muster.

"You call *that* acting?" Dr. Penny laughs. "Whew!" she says, rolling her eyes.

"Stow it, Eggers," he fires back, and we're off again to medical. Almost there. Gabriel's legs pump along next to us, seemingly unfazed by fatigue. He's the only one not panting.

Moloch is in him. I know it.

We've got to get him out of him – and banish him.

Hold on, Aadhya. Almost time.

"What is the meaning of all of this?" Dr. Canterbury asks. "Who are all you people?"

I catch sight of Elias, strapped to a gurney with all kinds of motion-limiting contraptions. He's wired up to an EKG, and its slow steady beeps sound out loud and clear. My own heart goes out to him. He didn't ask for this. But then Elias catches sight of Gabriel. "Gabriel!" he shouts with joy. "Brother!" His face contorts into wild, unrestrained gladness at the sight of his brother.

"Hello, twin!" Gabriel says, equally as joyful, seemingly oblivious of the gravity of the situation. It's like he's forgotten he's in cuffs.

"Where are you at, Doc?" Whitmire growls.

"With what?" the doctor asks, glancing around wildly as a horde of us move into his domain, shifting things around, placing Gabriel on an adjacent gurney, still cuffed. "What is this?" he cries. "Stop that, don't touch that, and – hey! Leave that alone, what are you doing?" The doctor frantically tries to protect his tools and base of operations.

"With the regimen you gave him!" Whitmire yells.

"Uh, I – I don't know! Maybe another fifteen minutes," Dr. Canterbury whimpers back in frustration. "It's wearing off right now anyway and *hey*! What are you guys *doing* anyway?"

"Fifteen minutes," Whitmire grumbles. "Holy hell." He wipes the sweat from his brow. Dark circles line both of his armpits. "What about this one?" he asks, pointing over at Gabriel. Elias' twin's eyes have grown darker or – something. His eye sockets seem to have sunken, and the dark tissue underneath is appealing for visibility. He spasms with his Tourette's, momentarily.

"What about him?" Dr. Canterbury asks, and it's then that he realizes Gabriel is Elias' twin. In the hysteria of the influx of visitors, he had missed it. "Hey, what is this?" he asks, ping-ponging back and forth between both twins, unable to believe his eyes.

"Don't worry about him," I say. "He doesn't need a sedative or anything. He'll soon show what he's made of." I turn dark eyes upon Gabriel. He just stares right back at me, cryptically.

"Well, that's that. I guess we just wait," Whitmire says, coldly, and a hush falls over our group as they ponder what I just said. No one really knows what this whole exchange will look like. We're all just proceeding on trust now.

Elias' EKG continues to sound out, but the beeps are further apart now, stretching, separating into sleep patterns.

Gabriel gazes lovingly at Elias. "I'm so glad to be with you again, brother. To be with family," he says, and then once more he glances back over at me, his dark eyes glinting. I can't stand his stare: it's revolting. He doesn't have the right to look at or talk to me.

"Don't look at me, you filth," I hiss. He just smiles, smugly, once more, and then turns to face his brother again. "It's been a long time coming, has it not, brother?"

"Yes, it has," Elias agrees, and then he yawns.

Elias is yawning. Good! His body is through fighting the medicine, and succumbing to sleep. I quickly text Michael and ask if they're ready. He confirms they are.

"Move them side by side, please, Doctor," I ask Canterbury. "It's almost time."

"Yes, it's almost time," Gabriel breathes.

Dr. Canterbury shrugs, looking to Whitmire for his approval on the matter.

Whitmire nods. "Go ahead, please, doc."

The doctor does as he's instructed, wheeling Gabriel over next to Elias. Elias appears sleepy. So does Gabriel now, but his sleep is controlled; intentional. The twins are parallel to each other, and both turn to face each other.

Gabriel breathes a contented "Ahhhh, there he is. My family." Elias smiles sleepily at his twin as the drug wears off. He's been awake far longer than he should be.

"Gabriel…" he yawns.

"Elias…" Gabriel yawns back.

I quickly dial Michael Brickert, their unknown half-brother. *That's right. This* is *about* family, *you prick – and you're about to be reunited with Mom Brickert and then banished forever, Moloch.*

Michael answers. "Hey, Tracie. You ready?"

"Ready," I confirm.

"What – is the…?" Elias mutters, quickly slipping into a deep and deserved sleep. Gabriel emits a soft, sinister chuckle as he, too, fades.

I move over between them, handing the phone to Whitmire, standing next to me. It's a weird séance thing that I've got to do, but it's what Aadhya said to do. Despite the revulsion I feel, here goes.

I place a hand on each of their shoulders. Elias dimly, briefly reacts to my touch, his eyes briefly fluttering upward, and I'm reminded of when he was on the forest floor and I had to bring him back to Airway.

Gabriel, however… touching him is utterly revolting. I glance down and see him grinning up at me in a wicked sneer, his eyebrows raised as his eyes flutter.

"I feel them," Aadhya says through the phone. "Mmm, I feel them. Hello, sons."

Without surprise or delay, Gabriel replies "Hello, mother. So good to hear your voice." Aadhya does not reply.

Elias says nothing; he's losing consciousness fast, fading under the heavy curtain of fatigue held long at bay by modern medicine.

A flicker stabs through me: some faint stab of an energy strain or other, hitting my senses with a sharpness that words can't describe. I'm shocked and entranced as I stand still, waiting, listening to the lulling speech of Aadhya. She knows. She senses her sons, and she's speaking to us.

Gabriel watches his brother intently, though placidly, as Elias falls under, giving way to sleep, helpless against its tractor beam. Elias' EKG is morphing into a quiet, decades-apart blip, elasticized and lessening in strength as he dives into REM state.

Gabriel swallows, almost nervous-like, watching his twin with eager apprehension. I swear the bastard licks his lips at the oncoming entry point of tumult he was anticipating, and then he, too, closes his eyes.

I don't know any of the words, but it's some language I've never heard. Aadhya's voice rises and falls like waves of the sea, driven by the wind and then backing down, repelled by a defiant cliff face. She is rhythmic in her oration, speaking strange texts most likely long forgotten or buried, but now resurrected with power as she speaks to all of us, her gritty, raspy voice sounding loud and clear through the phone speaker.

I twitch with a sharp spasm. "You okay?" Whitmire asks me quietly, but his voice seems muted, distant, like an echo bouncing off a soft, faraway dream.

I've become some kind of conduit, channeling Aadhya's vocal power and the spirit within her words, bouncing between Gabriel, Elias and myself, reverberating and pounding back through me as a jet engine, then dimming to a nighttime whisper.

Memories flow through me of events I don't know or remember. Sights and scenes unfamiliar to me careen through my amygdala as I just try to hold on to both of them. I'm seeing their early memories. I see a young Aadhya smiling down upon a child. It looks to be Elias: he has softer features.

Flashes of light cascade through me as the memories tumble over me. I feel stabs and pinpricks of sensation. The hairs on my arms all stand up. Dylan's dim voice whispers to me. Rosie says something to me… I think it's "Breathe, Tracie." I try to. It feels hot.

Elias' EKG slows, and then stops. Gabriel breathes out in a long, drawn-out moan that sounds orgasmic.

Elias?

I can't feel him anymore.

And that's when I see Gabriel's tattoo – the strange swirls on his right bicep, once more: *hollow.* No longer with two figures intertwined and holding hands. No longer with two distinct figures blending formlessly into each other.

One brother remaining.

I try to say something as my vision grows blurry, but my mouth won't move.

Aadhya's voice grows in intensity, chanting bizarre incantations, rising as a tempest, and then subsiding into a calm breeze. She shouts and then whispers, rails and then coos. And through it all, I can no longer feel Elias.

The shoulder that my left hand is placed on – Elias' shoulder – feels icy cold to the touch now.

A steady *beeeeeeep* sounds through the room, echoing into a swampy reverb, blending into the tumult of voices all around me and the muted din of people scurrying in haste.

It's one of my lasting, final sensations before I pass out.

But I know with certainty what it means.

Elias is dead.

28: THE MISSING

The Past: ***Unknown***

I know him before I see him.

It's Gabriel's voice, yes, but I know the truth: it's really Moloch underneath that skin: his creepy, undulating voice beckons to me before I can pinpoint it. It seems to rise from my left and then pan to my right before falling out of hearing, but there's a following echo to everything he says: a stereo bounce delay that repeats all of his swampy voice, ricocheting off cavernous spaces whose outlines I cannot make out.

In fact, I can't see *anything* clearly. Dim hues of pastels and ambers, fiery colors and muted tones swirl all around me: nebulous and indistinguishable, like waking up from a stupor and you can't rub your eyes clean again. My feet don't appear to be fixed on any solid ground. I don't get it. I'm drifting… drifting… drifting somewhere in ethereal disconnect. And where is Dylan? Rosie? Penny? Dr. Canterbury?

I can no longer feel Elias. Oh, I feel Gabriel, and I feel Aadhya, but I no longer feel Elias. He is dead then, and that saddens me. But it was a risk we had to take in banishing Moloch, and I told myself very clearly that I had to let him go. That's still the truth.

There is a strange tumult of noise echoing just beyond the realm of hearing. I can't see clearly, but I can hear it, like dim concussions and exclamations, resounding out from some remote place above me.

The voice speaks again. "Greetings, Ms. Vossler," it says, chillingly.

Gabriel. I'm in here with him. Or… something.

"Thank you for doing exactly as Moloch wished," the chilling voice whispers to me, and a chill runs through me. "We know it was hard. I don't know how we can ever thank you." The voice emits a faint, grim chuckle.

"You can thank me by putting your own head between your own demon legs and kissing your own demon ass," I bite back, my head rotating frenetically, searching for him.

"Tsk, tsk," he chides, quietly. I'm glancing around in every direction, but I can't see him anywhere. The voice seems disembodied, stabbing out at me from various points. *Where is he???*

"You've been brought in here for a reason, Ms. Vossler. There was no other way to conduct the transfer other than to have both of us physically present – no glass between us – and to have Mother's chanting voice present as well. All of the elements needed to be present."

"What are you even saying, Moloch? Show yourself!"

"I'm saying, quite plainly, Ms. Vossler, that you were needed. You have been needed for a great while now, and it has saddened me to see us sundered so. We belong together."

"What?!" I scream at him. "You're a psychotic demon freak! Let me out!"

He doesn't stop. *I need you to listen to me, Tracie Vossler* bounces around loud as a jet engine, until I'm covering my ears with the wind kicking up and swirling around me in violent gusts and torrents.

"There was no real way Mother could successfully banish the unwanted presence, you understand. Not until we had all family present."

"Look, Moloch, I get it. You've got your little game you're playing. Your time is up, okay? Aadhya! Can you hear me? Go ahead please! What are you waiting for?"

"Tracie, you're not listening to me," Moloch insists, and it's a gentle, chilling whisper that jars me. "I said we needed *all family present.*"

My eyes squint, frustrated and impatient. What is Aadhya waiting for? "Aadhya!" I call out. There is no answer, and for the first time in here, I'm afraid. The temperature seems to drop by at least fifteen degrees, and a shrill gust bites at me. "Aadhya?" my voice calls out feebly, feeling for the first time very alone, bereft of help, with no one to hear me. "Michael! Anyone?"

Aadhya has been utterly silenced.

Help... comes the feeble whisper from my soul, calling out to no one.

"We've searched a long time, Tracie. A *long* time. Thirty-three years, to be exact. We're so glad we found you again. We thought you were dead, sister. All signs and reports said that you were, and a doctor even pronounced your time of death… the certificate even said so. Just like Mother!" he says. "Isn't that funny… you suffered cardiac arrest during childbirth, and everyone thought you were dead. They disposed of you in that cold meat locker, but I was able to gather you, to save you, and to allow you to live, Tracie. You were so beautiful."

I have no words. It's a trick. "You're lying!" I scream, but then my voice catches and the words don't fully sound out. My grief and horror drowns out my cry, and my heart is beating irregularly as I process what he's saying. I'm gutted, hollowed out at even the slimmest *suggestion* of such an insidious fantasy, but for some reason I can't speak any more. My voice has been silenced, and I'm powerless to answer him.

"It was a pure stroke of luck, don't you know? Your apparently undead newborn body being kidnapped by that morgue worker in secret, raised as their own, unbeknownst to any of us. It's still amazing.

"And then! Ahhh! Your being so stuck in grief at the loss of your *own* daughter that you traveled all the way to

Shoreline to meet Mother. Ha! No one could have predicted it. Well, except myself, of course. It was all part of the plan.

"The kidnapped daughter searching for her mother, and they meet. It's like the hall of mirrors all over again, but separated by thirty-three years. Mother's incantations proved useful after all."

I'm dizzying; I need to vomit, but there's no bile in here; this isn't a real stomach, and this isn't a real body anymore. I'm caught between the real and the dead, somewhere, with only Moloch to host me: my vile guide in this ethereal plain.

"You're such a fighter, Tracie. You always have been. That's why you survived. You keep pushing through, just like I do. *Pushing through.* You were the twin I should have had all along. Poor Elias, Tracie. Not very tough in the fiber, unfortunately, and too weak to do my bidding. Why, our dear Elias, he never even knew Mother was still alive. Poor boy. Had he known, had he actually *met* her again, he would have tried to stop Gabriel and I. But this was all for a greater plan, don't you see? All part of my plan. *Moloch's* plan. We thank you, Tracie."

The words of Dr. Penny sound out clearly in my head.

Well, suppose this demon is here purely for mischief and murder. Fine. So be it. That is its motivation. But could there be something else? Perhaps some part of a greater plan? Rarely have I ever encountered spiritual realms colliding when there wasn't something grand at stake. Perhaps the twins are part of a bigger picture that Moloch wishes you to bear witness to.

And then, with a thrill of horror rushing through me, I realize the terrible truth: I *am* the sister that supposedly died in childbirth. I am the *only* one who Aadhya could have used to connect her twins – no... *triplets!* – to conjoin all of us in the enchanting spell of her terrible Yogic magic.

Of course: *I'm family.*

Aadhya's words rush back at me now as well:

You're her, aren't you? The one that Elias loves.

Waterless tears flow from my eyes. Soundless heaves echo outward from my chest. Airless gasps croak out from my throat as I float here in wraithlike, nebulous nothingness. We all, the lot of us, played *right* into Moloch's hands, fulfilling his dastardly wishes and enabling him to continue his murderous streak.

I can't feel her...

I can't feel my Mother.

I hear Moloch inhale once more to bathe me in terror.

"And now, my dear sister, at last reunited for this purpose, I fear it is time to say goodbye forever to the unwanted presence," he says, and I'm silently weeping to myself, my body closed off to the possibility of tears. "For, now, it is time for me to take my place in Elias' body, and to shed the Earthly shell of Gabriel forever. No one will ever know! They've arrested Gabriel, but poor Gabriel died on that table in the prison medical quarters after being surrendered to their custody. And now, Elias will come back to life. Elias with *me* inside him, forever. I shall finish my twin's sentence in prison, and shall enjoy my continued recreation there.

"Which, unfortunately, leaves no further place for you, I'm afraid, because you died right there between us today. I'm so very sorry, Tracie," he says, completely devoid of any trace of pity or empathy. "I'm afraid that today it is *you* that must be banished."

"Wait!" I scream within my fading being, voiceless and toneless, summoning everything within me to get his attention; to delay his judgment. He appears to notice my struggle. Mercifully, my tongue feels loosened and I can feel my lungs gather air for speech once more. Panting, I summon up all the energy I can to make my appeal.

"Moloch," I plead. "I'm sorry. For everything. Please don't banish me. I will never interfere again. I promise you with every fiber of my being. Please have Mother send me into someone else so that I can still live with my daughter. Please. She's my everything. I can't lose her. She can't lose me. Surely you understand this. Surely you can show mercy to a mother who wants to save her daughter? Just like Mother wanted to save me. Please, Moloch. Save the Mother's daughter. Please."

The voice is silent in consideration. The winds swirl around me, whispering and racing in eddying, silent gusts.

The voice speaks.

"And even were I to grant someone to someone who so interfered with our plans, who would you even wish to enter?"

There's only one. I send the name to Mother, and she, to Moloch. It's a woman that has loved Lela like a mother. Someone who would continue to love her. Someone Lela would have the least amount of trouble accepting love from, and the one who knows her and has spent nearly as much time with her as her own real mother has. I feel terrible for doing it – for even *thinking* it – but I must. I *must* do it! Lela needs someone. Concepción would surely understand… wouldn't she? And she's lived a long life already… right?

Lela needs Conchita, our sweet Concepción. Me.

I can practically hear Moloch smile, grimly chuckling to himself. "A scheming choice. This would place you in close proximity to your daughter, while simultaneously delivering you from any further legal jeopardy, being dead, of course. I commend you on your cunning… it's almost as good as mine."

"What will happen to Concepción?" I ask.

"She will sleep in perfect peace, having been delivered from the travails of this life," he assures me.

No problemo. You have to do the hard thing, I'm here for you. You know that. Her sweet words ring out at me. She could not have meant this… not in a million years. But I hope she will understand.

Oh, Conchita, I'm so sorry. I'm so, so sorry!

I voice no dissent. I can't. My mouth is closed once more, and it's as if a lock has snapped shut. I've made my choice, and that's that. Moloch knows who Concepción is. He's familiar with our family. He may have even had our dear Conchita drive Lela to the water tower herself, while Lela was asleep; she would have trusted her Conchita and would not have fought. And then, there, Moloch imprisoned her.

"It shall be done," he concludes.

The lulling voice of Aadhya starts to reverberate around me, a tremulous chant growing in strength and intensity, invoking foreign words with potency to do Moloch's bidding; her frail, elderly self can no longer fight back, poor woman.

And then, her voice stills, and with that disconnect I know she's asleep once more, expended of energy. Perhaps she's even dead. But not before she did what she set out to do: 'banish the unwanted presence,' she said.

The unwanted presence. *Me.*

The wind subsides. The colors fade. The sound drains. My body floats freely, and I see it now: drifting into miniscule form, away from me, diminishing… receding into the distance as blackness was, is, and always will be in here, where blackness is all.

And then, suddenly, I'm at home, waking up suddenly as if from a stark nightmare, except I know everything…I remember everything.

I waste no time, throwing myself up off the couch with my weak knees; hurling myself into the bathroom, panting.

I stare at myself in the mirror and breathe deeply of the strong fragrance of *Estee Lauder White Linen*. I'm in tears. She's been banished to God knows where so that I can live on.

It's been done.

Hasta la próxima, Conchita. Instead of my Honda Fit, I get her navy blue Nissan Altima and her body, and she gets nothing. I weep at the trade.

Poor Conchita, dead, so that I could live.

I know her before I even see her.

29: THE ADOPTION

Present: **Sunday, January 16th 2021**

It's almost like living.

I've adopted a new body, and I've adopted a daughter, even though she was mine to begin with.

It hasn't been easy, however: none of it.

I've proven myself over and over again, through and through, but there's nothing for Lela to articulate other than various expressions of disbelief and awe.

Oh, she wept. Long and sad, she wept. I wept as well; we dearly miss our Conchita, and though it's an uneasy replacement for her mom, she's starting to understand that I did what I had to do. She's understandably jarred and saddened.

And how can I blame her? I have only myself to blame. All of that body-swapping by Gabriel and Elias that so turned me off? I ended up doing the same thing, so now I'm just as guilty – and as bad – as Gabriel and Elias themselves.

Spoken like a true Brickert, I think to myself.

Airway Heights never was the same after all that. I think they might close it down and build a new one. Moloch continued his killing fields there, but then he moved on, presumably to other penitentiaries or other hunting grounds where fear is maximized and his prey can't readily escape. How he got into another body, or where he roams now, I have no idea, and I don't really care, as long as I can be with my Lela.

I live now with the knowledge of the evil atrocities that I've committed, the greatest of them murder. I murdered my dear Concepción, all in the name of my own conception within her, simply in order to escape eternal banishment and oblivion and be with my daughter. I escaped legal jeopardy because, according to Dr. Penny's clinical terminology, all of it is 'codswallop.' No one knows it's really me in here, and it's a lie that Lela and I must carefully guard for as long as we live.

I don't reach out to Michael Brickert or his wife Steph. I have no intention of doing so. *I think he was the bad guy all along. I think he had a demon in him.* Those were Michael's words, and I can't bear to bring the news to him that he was utterly mistaken; it was his dear mother all along, the Yogic Hindu witch who screwed everything up and still lives under his roof. But I don't feel her anymore, and I'm truly convinced that she's finally dead.

Thus ends that Yogic nightmare.

It has taken the greatest effort to purge everything from my mind and take on the mantle of our sweet Conchita. I'm my daughter's mother *and* her babysitter. I'm old enough now to be her grandmother. I probably won't even get to see her own children grow and live. It's a desperate trade-off that I've made: a Faustian bargain, a deal with the devil… but I did it for her.

I'm just not sure she'll ever see it that way. I don't blame her. It's a lot to take, and a lot of craziness to swallow without any trace of doubt or even marginal skepticism.

Detective Gaskill interviewed me after the complete disappearance of Airway Heights Security Guard Tracie Vossler; she just had no idea I was standing right in front of her the whole time. I must have perfected my Latin accent by now.

Warden Caleb Canton is back at his post, and he's visited us to pay his respects to my daughter and offer his condolences on the death of her mom. Lela has the hardest time with it, of course, knowing full well that her mother is alive, preserved in a full-on body-swap.

All of this could make someone go completely crazy, and, frankly, maybe the thought of banishing me from my own body into Concepción's – and the ensuing psychological mayhem that it is currently wreaking on both of us – gave Moloch great pleasure to envision. I suppose it still gives him great pleasure, knowing that my old form is no longer mine, and that involving myself in his affairs cost me something great.

Poor Michael Brickert had no idea he was living with a witch who never outgrew being a witch. Who never outgrew evil. I pray for them, as best as I can. It's perfectly clear to me now that Aadhya wanted this all along. That she had her own son kill her own husband, Kieran.

That she loved her Gabriel, her firstborn twin, over her second born twin, Elias. That she favored him.

That she resented her daughter for dying, for eluding them all this time, and for interfering with her plans.

That she banished Elias from this world and body-swapped Moloch into his, perhaps to rid Moloch of Gabriel's Tourette's syndrome and that identifying stigma. Who knows. But now Gabriel's 'Elias' body can go where it wants and do what it wishes. I shudder at the notion.

And finally, that she banished *me* from my very own body. After all, I'm the sister that never existed, and now truly doesn't anymore. I'm the daughter that died, and is born again as the daughter no longer. I'm the babysitter slash mom slash fugitive from justice who just wanted to do the right thing, but maybe yearned just a little too much. Dr. Penny would definitely agree with that assessment, at least.

And Rosie? Not sure how much her prayers actually helped. Maybe she's one of those 'prayer warriors', but perhaps God was on vacation the day she prayed for me, because now, I'm adrift, living out in my days in a borrowed form with a stolen name, and it was all of my own doing.

Moloch got what he wanted, as I suppose he always has down through the ages. Now he gets to finish Elias' prison sentence in his body and commit as many more murders as his wicked heart desires.

It's a freaking conundrum, and it always will be.

Life isn't the same anymore, nor could it be.

In fact, it's just this side of dying.

THE END

AFTERWORD

A Christian author writing outright horror? Perish the thought!

The very sentence is so nonconformist and diametrically opposed to anything I've ever written. But I just had to do it. An author needs to stretch themselves, yes?

I knew that I didn't want to write The Exorcist or anything like that, but I did know that I wanted to write something that would be moving, have redemption and heart, and create a sense of horror and dread. I touched on this especially in a single chapter of *Dissonance Volume I: Reality* – and the *Dissonance* saga is in and of itself a flavor of horror as well – but I didn't plumb the depths, as it were. Thus, this novel.

…and the next one! There's yet another horror novel up my sleeve after this one, and I'm excited to commence it as soon as I'm done with *Blood Echoes*.

The main character in this novel is someone who desperately wants to do what is right, but becomes immersed in pollution and a diluted and contaminated sense of morality.

And, to that end, I didn't want to end on a happy note. This is, after all, a horror novel, and things don't always pan out at the end of the show in such genres. I appreciated writing from a dual timeline, and if you reread the book now, little things like Tracie's car vs. Tracie's Altima will stand out to you. It isn't apparent until the end that she got Conchita's car, because that could only exist in the later timeline, in retrospect. I hope you enjoyed the jumps back and forth in time as the older 2021 Concepción looked back on the younger Tracie's journey through all of 2020.

Thank you to the person who wishes to remain anonymous who helped me with knowledge on the inner workings of Airway

Heights Penitentiary and the protocol and processes that go on behind prison walls. I could not have done it without you!

Thank you to my beloved wife and editor, Janine with *Denouement Editing*, my adored ARC readers Victoria Richmond, Jeannine Dryden, Sherry Camp and Walker Armstrong, and to my highly esteemed ALC listeners Rhonda Davis, Vance Pease, Katarzyna Drake-Rookwood, and Victoria Richmond. I SO appreciate you and all your help with all of my books!

Thank you to ALL of my readers the world over. I would not be able to do this without you. Thank you for helping me get my own darkness within *without*, and share it with the world. Each new story is a gift, each new finished book is a celebration, and each new reader is a relationship I highly cherish.

You are all SO appreciated!

With love,

Aaron Ryan

ABOUT THE AUTHOR

Award-winning and bestselling author, speaker, panelist, workshop presenter, business coach and voice actor Aaron Ryan lives in Washington with his wife and two sons, along with Macy the dog, Winston the cat, and those two crazy finches Frodo & Sam (yes, we've cycled through a few of them. ☹)

He is the prolific author of the bestselling *Dissonance* 6-book alien invasion saga, the Christian dystopian fiction trilogy *The End*, the *Talisman* trilogy, the sci-fi thrillers *Forecast*, *The Slide*, *Blood Echoes* and *The Phoenix Experiment*, the nonfiction books *You are my whole Earth: A Daddy's love for his Sons, God Is Not Santa, You're Going Straight To Helen (In A Handbasket)* and *Aaron Ryan presents "A Lyrical Empirical Satirical Miracle,"* the children's picture books *The Ring of Truth*, *The Sword of Joy* and *The Book of Power*, *The Super Ordinary Heroes Series: Empathy, The Invisibility Cloak* and *The Time-Stopping Hug,* the business reference books *How to Successfully Self-Publish & Promote Your Self-Published Book* and *The Superhero Anomaly*, 6 business books on voiceovers penned under his former stage name (Joshua Alexander), as well as a previous fictional novel, *The Omega Room.*

When he was in second grade, he was tasked with writing a creative assignment: a fictional book. And thus, *The Electric Boy* was born: a simple novella full of intrigue, fantasy, and 7-year-old wits that electrified Aaron's desire to write. From that point forward, Aaron evolved into a creative soul that desired to create.

He enjoys the arts, media, music, performing, poetry, and being a daddy. In his lifetime he has been an author, voiceover artist, wedding videographer, stage performer, musician, producer, rock/pop artist, executive assistant, service manager, paperboy, CSR, poet, tech support, worship leader, and more. The diversity of his life experiences gives him a unique approach to business, life, ministry, faith, and entertainment.

Aaron's favorite author by far is J.R.R. Tolkien, but he also enjoys Suzanne Collins, James S.A. Corey, Michael Crichton, Marie Lu, Madeleine L'Engle, John Grisham, Tom Clancy, Tim Lebbon, Christopher Golden, C.S. Lewis, Stephen King and Dave Barry.

Aaron has always had a passion for storytelling. Visit his website at https://www.authoraaronryan.com, feel free to join his exclusive and private group on Facebook at https://authoraaronryangroup.com, or check out his store at https://authoraaronryanstore.com.

Aaron is interviewed often and is on Podmatch.com. Be sure to check out Aaron's wide selection of podcast appearances at https://www.youtube.com/playlist?list=PLMnbc3h716bs6u4j5B4B31DIsoBLkktwM.

Thank you for considering and following Aaron Ryan!

REVIEWS

If you liked this or any of my books, please visit the Amazon and Goodreads pages for the specific book(s) and leave a positive review. Once it shows up, email the screenshot to aaron@authoraaronryan.com please, for a discount on your next book purchase from me!

Thank you so much, from the bottom of my heart. Reviews really do help a ton, and I'm so very grateful to you for taking the time. You didn't have to – which makes me all the more glad that you did.

Blessings!
-Aaron Ryan

CONNECT WITH AARON

Feel free to check out the following links:

Subscribe to Aaron's blog for free giveaways, news and new releases at **authoraaronryan.com/blog**

Subscribe to Aaron's Substack at
authoraaronryan.substack.com/

Join the Author Aaron Ryan Facebook community at
facebook.com/groups/authoraaronryan

Subscribe to Aaron's YouTube channel at
youtube.com/@authoraaronryan

Visit Aaron's social media links to connect with him at
dot.cards/authoraaronryan

Visit Aaron's website at authoraaronryan.com

Follow Aaron on IMDb at imdb.me/authoraaronryan

ALSO BY THE AUTHOR

As Aaron Ryan:

1. *Dissonance Volume I: Reality*
2. *Dissonance Volume II: Reckoning*

3. *Dissonance Volume III: Renegade*
4. *Dissonance Volume IV: Relentless*
5. *Dissonance Volume Zero: Revelation*
6. *Dissonance Volume Up: Rising*
7. *The Complete Dissonance Alien Invasion Saga*
8. *THE END: Alpha*
9. *THE END: Omicron*
10. *THE END: Omega*
11. *The Complete THE END Christian Dystopian Saga*
12. *Forecast*
13. *The Slide*
14. *The Phoenix Experiment*
15. *Thrillerumvirate*
16. *Blood Echoes*
17. *Talisman: Subterfuge*
18. *Talisman: Nexus*
19. *Talisman: Halcyon*
20. *The Complete Talisman Series*
21. *The Ring of Truth*
22. *The Sword of Joy*
23. *The Book of Power*
24. *The Christian Kids Values, Identity & Affirmation Series*
25. *You are my whole Earth: A Daddy's love for his Sons*
26. *God Is Not Santa*
27. *You're Going Straight To Helen (In A Handbasket)*
28. *A Lyrical Empirical Satirical Miracle*
29. *Examining The Lord of the Rings: An independent critique by Aaron Ryan*
30. *The Superhero Anomaly*

31. *How to Successfully Self-Publish & Promote Your Independent Book: A Self-Publishing & Business Marketing Guide For The Independent Author*
32. *Reflections: A Compilation of Journals and Poetry*
33. *The Omega Room (abandoned in the early 90's)*
34. *Autobiography (no longer available)*
35. *Glimmerings – works of poetry*

As his former stage name, Josh Alexander:

36. *Voiceovers: A Super Business, A Super Life*
37. *Voiceovers: A Super Fun Pursuit*
38. *Voiceovers: A Super Responsibility*
39. *Running a Successful Voiceover Business*
40. *How do I get started in Voiceovers?*
41. *Five T's to Triumph: The Secrets to Getting Cast in Voiceovers*

Gratitude is a hallmark of our home. At my wedding, I was labeled by my cousin as a "rabid over-thanker."

I have no such intention of losing this esteemed reputation.

So, with that, once again, THANK YOU – rabidly – *each* and *every* one of you – for reading my books, and for leaving reviews online about them, and for telling your friends and family about them. Really, thank you from the deepest and warmest places in my heart.

Made in the USA
Coppell, TX
19 May 2026

77535285R00184